GOLDEN FILLY SERIES

CALL FOR COURAGE

LAURAINE SNELLING

BETHANY HOUSE PUBLISHERS
MINNEAPOLIS, MINNESOTA 55438

Cover illustration by Brett Longley

Published by Bethany House Publishers
A Ministry of Bethany Fellowship, Inc.
6820 Auto Club Road, Minneapolis, Minnesota 55438

Printed in the United States of America

Library of Congress Cataloging-in-Publication Data

Snelling, Lauraine.
  Call for courage / Lauraine Snelling.
     p. cm. — (Golden filly series ; bk. 5)
  Summary: After her history-making Kentucky Derby win, Trish
believes she can go on to win the triple crown of thoroughbred racing
but untold adversity and near tragedy may stop her progress.
  [1. Horse racing—Fiction. 2. Family problems—Fiction.
3. Christian life—Fiction.]
I. Title. II. Series: Snelling, Lauraine. Golden filly series ; bk. 5.
PZ7.S677cal   1992
[Fic]—dc20   92-16240
                                               CIP
ISBN 1-55661-260-5   AC

To Ruby MacDonald and Pat Rushford,
my first dedicated critique group
and lasting friends.

We owe each other our successes.

LAURAINE SNELLING is a full-time writer who has authored several published books, sold articles for a wide range of magazines, and written weekly features in local newspapers. She also teaches writing courses and trains people in speaking skills. She and her husband, Wayne, have two grown children and make their home in California.

Her lifelong love of horses began at age five with a pony named Polly and continued with Silver, Kit, Rowdy, and her daughter's horse Cimeron, which starred in her first children's book *Tragedy on the Toutle*.

CHAPTER 1

This was turning out to be a year of firsts. First race, first win, first trip to California, and now the first female to win the Kentucky Derby. Sixteen-year-old Tricia Evanston hugged the tall, black colt she and her father had raised and trained. Spitfire lived up to his name.

Back at Churchill Downs on Sunday morning, Trish still rode the high from yesterday's win. Their dream had come true. She and Spitfire had won the Kentucky Derby!

"Spitfire, you crazy horse, stop it now." Trish tried to insert at least a hint of command in her tone but failed miserably. *Serious* just didn't seem to fit into her vocabulary this morning. The laughter kept bubbling, joined by giggles.

Spitfire might be the newly crowned winner of the Kentucky Derby, but he loved hats—as in flipping them off favored people's heads. This morning, the flying hat of fedora vintage belonged to assistant trainer Patrick O'Hern.

"You should see the look on your face," Trish said, smiling at the more than slightly rounded ex-jockey. A halo of white hair fringed his shiny bald head.

"I'll put me a look on 'is face!" Patrick leaned over to grab his hat, but a playful breeze joined in the prank, bowling the grungy hat a step or three across the gravel.

Trish leaned against the wall of barn 41, her legs feeling like cooked spaghetti from all the laughing.

David kept a wary eye on the black colt and a hand on his favorite Seattle Mariner's baseball cap as he reached for Patrick's dust-covered hat.

"You know, if you two were wearing Runnin' On Farm hats, he'd leave you alone," Trish said. "He knows those hats are in his honor."

David gave her one of his smart-big-brother to dumb-little-sister looks. "Why don't you just get up on him and work off some of his orneriness?"

Trish tossed the reins she held over the animal's black head and turned for a leg-up. Patrick gave her the boost. Trish let her legs dangle below the stirrups as she gathered her reins. "Y'all see if you can stay out of trouble now, ya he-ah?" Her laughter floated back on the breeze as she nudged her horse into a trot.

Trish and Spitfire stopped beside the track entry. She watched other horses coming and going as she slid her feet into the iron stirrups. With hands crossed on the colt's withers, she kept her reins collected but at rest.

Spitfire, head raised, sniffed the morning scents of horse, damp sand, sweat, and the lingering aroma of the crowds from the day before. He blew, nostrils flaring with the force.

If Trish closed her eyes she could still see and hear the cheering spectators. Even though it had been pouring rain, she and Spitfire had taken their bow. What a feeling—to win the Kentucky Derby on the colt bred on their own farm!

"Can't ya just see it all," a familiar voice interrupted her daydreaming. Red Holloran, with hair that gave him the nickname and a smile to melt any female heart, sat on the back of a dark bay. He gazed around the track with Trish. "Never thought you'd do it after that start."

"We Evanstons don't give up easily." Trish nudged Spitfire forward. They turned counterclockwise on the track and walked their horses side by side along the outer rail.

"I noticed. You see the morning paper?"

"Nope."

"You'll love your picture." Red grinned at her.

"I'll bet. Monster from the mud lagoon. They shoulda made me take a shower before I got on the scale. Coming from behind on a sloppy track like that one—" Trish shook her head. "If a person didn't know we wore crimson and gold silks, they never would have been able to tell yesterday, at least not from my front. And Spitfire was just as bad." She leaned forward to stroke the horse's arched neck. "Weren't ya, fella?" Spitfire pulled at the bit, a gentle tug that politely begged for more than a walk.

Trish obliged and posted to a lazy jog.

"How do ya like that new car?" Red kept pace.

"My mother is going to have a fit." Trish shook her head. "Can you see me—at sixteen—tooling around Vancouver, Washington—where it rains three hundred days out of the year—in a bright red Chrysler LeBaron convertible?" Trish settled back in the saddle. "She'll have a cow."

"Your mother seems like a real nice lady to me."

"She is. But she's not your mother. And you're not her only daughter. The daughter she'd much rather see not racing thoroughbreds."

"Well, she can't make you give the car back."

"No, but she can keep me from driving it."

"Would she?"

"I don't know." Trish frowned. "We haven't always gotten along the best. She and I—well, we have different ideas of what I should do with my life."

"What do you want to do?"

"Ride, race." Trish glanced up to the empty stands where a couple of men in green and white uniforms cleaned up trash. "To keep on doing what I'm doing—full-time."

"And your mother?"

"She wants me to go to school, get good grades, and go on to college—also with good grades, so I can have a good, safe life."

"Nothing wrong with that."

Trish raised her eyebrows at Red. "Would you?"

"No. But it *is* important to finish school."

Trish sighed. "I know." She turned Spitfire off toward the barn. "See ya later."

"When do you leave for Baltimore?" Red raised his voice.

"Thursday, I think," Trish yelled back. She felt her butterflies take an experimental leap when she thought of the race ahead. Baltimore, Maryland. Home of Pimlico Race Course, where the Preakness Stakes was the next jewei in the Triple Crown of thoroughbred horseracing. The Derby was the first, the Preakness in two weeks, and the Belmont two weeks later.

"David?" Trish asked in the car on the way back to the hotel. They'd left Patrick grooming Spitfire, his hat hung safely on a nail in the tackroom.

"What?"

"Has Mom said anything about the car?" Trish concentrated on her driving, trying to sound casual. She could feel David studying her. "Well?"

"You mean your convertible?"

"You know that's what I mean; don't be difficult."

"I wouldn't plan on driving it to school every day, and it's a good thing you have money to pay the insurance. Other than that, I think she's kind of waiting to see what'll happen."

"What do you mean, what'll happen?"

"What she said was, 'I absolutely refuse to worry about Trish driving around in a red convertible until I have to.' "

Trish saw the humor in that. Her mother was trying very hard not to worry anymore. But as she had said, worrying was as much a part of her nature as the color of her eyes.

Trish was also beginning to understand about worry. It was an easy habit to fall into. But as her little voice kept reminding her, worry and faith didn't go well together.

"We were beginning to think you got lost," her father said when the two young people entered the family hotel suite. Hal glanced at his watch. "We're meeting Grandpa and Grandma at the restaurant in half an hour. The Finleys are coming too, so you'd better hustle."

"You see the papers?" Trish didn't wait for an answer when she spotted the opened newspapers on the coffee table. "Oh, yuck!" She stared from the picture back to her father. "I look awful. You can hardly even tell it's me."

David looked over her shoulder. "Looks like you took a mud bath. Hey, we oughta blow these up poster size."

Trish jabbed him in the gut with her elbow. "Sure, highlight of my life and I'm covered with mud. And Spitfire's not any better." She studied the pictures again and wrinkled her nose in distaste. "These *would* be in color, too."

"Well, the trophy's shiny and the roses are red; what more could you ask for?" Hal handed her another paper. "The articles are good but you'll have to read them later. The grands are leaving for home today so we need to spend what time we can with them."

Trish nearly bumped into the wall as she read one article on the way to the bathroom. The headline "First Female to Win the Roses" gave her goosebumps. She plugged in the curling iron, washed, then brushed her teeth. As she brushed she studied the face in the mirror. Hazel eyes, like her mother's, remained the same. Determined chin, only more so. Though her bangs were smashed flat from her helmet, the hot iron would take care of that. Her hair still curled just above her shoulders if she left it loose. *You'd think there'd be a difference after the big win yesterday*, she thought.

Trish pulled a summer-green cotton sweater over her head and stepped into a pair of white jeans. Three rolls with the iron, a brush job, hair clipped back, and she was ready. No time for makeup. She'd already heard her father making noises like they were late.

They ate at a fish house that overlooked the broad Ohio River. Just upriver they could see a paddlewheeler docked.

"I wish we could have eaten there," Trish pointed to the newly painted white vessel. "Wouldn't it be fun to cruise down the river like they did in the old days?"

"You'd have hated all the skirts and petticoats," Marge reminded her. "And the parasols. Just think how many dresses and skirts you *don't* wear now."

Trish nodded at her mother. "You're right." She stared at the glistening boat again. "But still . . ."

They had all served themselves at the elaborate buffet and returned to the room they'd reserved. It was both private and had a sweeping view of the river. Everyone sat at one long table, with Hal at the head.

"You sure pulled off a good one yesterday," Adam Finley, a horse owner and trainer from Central California, told Trish as he pulled out his chair and sat across from her. She'd gotten to know Adam and his wife on the trip to Santa Anita in April. "I thought Martha would squeeze my arm to death when that black colt of yours reared in the starting gate."

"He doesn't like thunder." Trish shuddered at the memory. It hadn't been one of her better moments, either.

"I don't know how you can get out there like that, with all that danger around you. Why, one jockey was ridden right into the rail." Trish's grandmother, Gloria Johnson, shook her head. A frown creased her forehead as she looked from Marge to Hal as if they'd lost their wits. "To think you'd let your daughter . . ."

Her husband, David, interrupted with a smile. "Now, dear, you promised."

In the last few days Trish had really begun to understand where her mother got the worry habit. It was obviously an inherited trait.

Trish looked up in time to catch a wink from her father. He'd been reading her mind again. Trish checked to see how her mother was reacting.

Marge was shaking her head. She rolled her eyes heavenward when she caught Trish's questioning look.

Trish pressed her lips together to keep a grin from

breaking out. Her mom had caught on.

"So, Trish," Adam Finley said, leaning across the table. "How about coming down and riding for me this summer? You remember we talked about it in April?"

How could she forget? What a dream it would be to race again in California. But at the same time she wished she could get the man to lower his voice. She stole a peek at her mother. She'd heard all right. Her frown said it all.

"I—uh, of course I remember. I'm just not sure what we're doing yet."

"Trish, you promised to make up that chemistry class this summer." Marge's tone didn't offer any outs.

Adam looked from Trish to her mother. "I see."

"Now you've stuck your foot in your mouth," Adam's wife, Martha, who appeared everyone's image of the perfect grandmother, scolded her husband. "You get so excited, you think everyone should think like you do."

"Well," Adam paused. "Trish *is* an amazing rider for one so young. I like the way she handles horses."

"Thank you," Trish responded. Her mother didn't look one bit happy.

"We'll see what we can work out," Hal said as he pushed his chair back. "And now, I have some announcements to make."

As soon as all eyes were on him he began, "First, congratulations, Trish. You have no idea how proud I am of you and Spitfire. Yesterday, you made one of my dreams come true. Thank you."

Trish could feel the heat blazing into her cheeks when everyone began applauding. She chewed her lip, then rose and took a quick bow. "Thanks, everybody." She could feel tears swimming at the back of her eyes at the look of love and pride on her father's face. Trish tried to blink them back and almost made it. "I thought all my tears ran out yesterday."

"Somehow *I* never seem to run out." Marge blew her nose and sniffed again.

Chuckles, like dry leaves before a wind, blew around the table.

"And secondly, BlueMist Farms has offered to buy shares in Spitfire with the agreement that he will retire to stud there. Two other people want in, too, so I'll have a lawyer draw up the papers and Spitfire will be legally syndicated, if that is okay with everyone."

"If I'm not one of those people you mentioned, I'd like in on the syndication, too," Adam said. "You just tell me your price per share and how many you'll offer."

"We'll work something out." Hal nodded. "I'd be pleased to have you in with us, Adam."

Trish heard the exchange with one part of her brain, but the other part was in shock. So soon? She hadn't thought of the colt leaving home till sometime in the far distant future. And then, not really. But many farms retired a stud colt after winning the Derby. And Spitfire carried good lines. His father, Seattle Slew, won the Triple Crown in 1977.

But Spitfire was hers. How could she let him go? And no one else could ride him. He wouldn't let anyone. Trish chewed on her thumbnail. She hadn't thought about Spitfire leaving Runnin' On Farm.

"You know we're not set up for a stud farm," David whispered in her ear.

"I know." Trish took a deep breath. "I just hadn't thought about it."

"You okay, Tee?" Hal had picked up her distress.

Trish nodded. She squared her shoulders but she didn't dare look directly at her father. She knew she'd break into tears right there.

"Think about Miss Tee," David added.

A smile tickled the corner of Trish's mouth. The little filly that had been born on her birthday always brought a happy reaction in her. At eight months, Miss Tee was just beginning her training.

"As I was saying earlier, I just don't understand why Trish—"

"Now, Mother . . ." Grandpa Johnson patted his wife's hand. He checked his watch. "I really think we'd better get on the road. I hate to leave you all, but I don't drive after dark anymore and Florida is a ways off. So thank you for a good time and this fine meal." He pulled out his wife's chair after he stood. "Come on, Mother. Let's get all the hugging and crying done so we can be going."

Trish pushed back her own chair. "Sorry I didn't get to spend more time with you," she said as she gave her grandfather a big hug. "Thanks for coming."

"You too, Grandma," she added. "Maybe you'll fly up for Pimlico. That's not too far away from Florida." Trish hugged the gray-haired woman who was short like herself.

"I don't know, dear. Watching you up on that black horse of yours nearly worried me to death. Now, you be careful." She stepped back and shook her head.

"I will, I promise," Trish said.

The Finleys left for the airport soon after the Evanstons waved off the departing grandparents. Hal had his arms around both Marge and Trish as they all stood in the parking lot waving goodbye.

"Well, let's get back to the hotel. We have a lot to do

before we leave tomorrow," Hal said.

"I thought we were leaving for Pimlico on Thursday." Trish looked up at her father.

"We are. But I have to fly home to Vancouver for a chemotherapy treatment. Your mother is going with me and we plan to be back on Wednesday."

"But, I thought . . ." Trish started to say. Her little nagging voice didn't give her a chance to finish. *No, you weren't thinking at all. Not about your father and the cancer. You just think about horse racing.*

CHAPTER 2

"I wish Dad were still here." Trish flopped back on her bed on Monday morning.

"Well, he's not and you're wasting time." David whirled around and headed for the door.

"What's the matter with you?"

"Nothing!"

"Right." Trish grabbed her windbreaker and trotted after him. David nearly ran to the elevator, or at least it seemed that way to Trish. *I didn't oversleep. No one's called. What set him off?* Trish's mind played with the questions while she studied the stern profile of her usually easygoing brother as they waited for the hotel elevator.

"Let's take the stairs." David wheeled to the right and pushed open the exit door. As they clattered down six flights of stairs, Trish's mind took up the game again. Even the set of David's shoulders declared his—anger? Resentment? Disgust? Trish wasn't sure. Just keeping up was effort enough.

"Okay, what is it?" She crossed her arms over her chest after snapping her seat belt in the rental car.

David's sigh sounded as if it had been trapped inside long enough to build up steam. "Does it ever occur to you that sometimes I get tired of being in charge?"

18

Trish was taken aback. "No. I mean, I guess I thought we kinda shared that, the responsibility and all. It's not like Dad does this on purpose. Leaving, I mean." She felt as if her words and thoughts rattled together and came out broken. "Besides, we have Patrick now."

"I know." David gripped the top of the steering wheel and leaned his forehead on his hands. "I guess part of it is this awful feeling I have in the pit of my stomach."

"Awful feeling? About what? Did Dad say something to you before they left this morning? I just gave them a hug and fell back to sleep."

"I don't know. No, nothing was said. Maybe it's just Dad's leaving us here."

"At least you don't have to talk with that guy from *Sports Illustrated* again. All by yourself."

"I'll be there if you need me," David reminded his sister.

"I meant without Dad. He always says exactly the right thing. I sound like someone with half a brain."

"Well, the article *is* mostly about you and Spitfire. Besides, you know what kind of questions they'll ask. Think of your answers in advance."

Trish nodded. Silence fell while they both looked out the window of the car. A flicker of red caught Trish's eye as a scarlet cardinal lighted on one of the blossom-frosted branches of the dogwood tree in front of them.

"Look," Trish whispered. "Halfway up the tree on the right." She breathed a sigh of delight as a dull-colored female joined her mate on the branch. The little male glistened like a ruby jewel set among the creamy blossoms.

"Well, we better get going." David reached for the ignition key and then paused. "We'd better be praying, Tee."

"For what? Right now things are going pretty smooth."

"I don't know, but I have a feeling." David turned his head to back the car out of the parking space. "A bad feeling."

Trish mentally sorted through her favorite Bible verses. They were printed on 3 x 5 cards and tacked above her desk at home. Her father had started the collection during his first hospital stay the previous fall. Finally she settled on "In everything give thanks." It was hard to pray when she didn't know what to pray for.

What if you really don't like what's coming? her nagging little voice inquired. *Then you're going to feel pretty stupid giving thanks for it.* Some days her inner voice seemed to be a help, but more often it nagged at her— like today.

Glad for the reprieve, Trish leaped from the car as soon as David parked beside Stakes barn 41, near their stall. A silver and blue horse van was stationed in the road waiting to load. The sounds of an early-morning track were music to Trish's ears. Horses nickering, a sharp whinny, people laughing, the rhythmic grunts of a galloping horse counterpoint with pounding hooves on the dirt track, a bird warbling his sunrise song in one of the gigantic oak trees.

Spitfire nickered as soon as he heard Trish greet Patrick. He tossed his head, spraying her with drops from his recent drink, then wuffled her hair and nosed her hands for the carrot she always carried. Trish gave him his treat and scratched behind his ears and down his cheek. The colt leaned his head against her chest and closed his eyes in bliss.

"If I didn't know better, I'd say you'll be a-spoilin'

him rotten." Patrick shook his head, but his smile told Trish that he understood the special relationship she and Spitfire shared. "Come on, old son," Patrick slipped into the stall and saddled the colt with practiced ease. "You be in bad need of a good run."

Trish fitted the headstall over the soft black ears and buckled the chin strap. Spitfire answered a whinny from a horse a few stalls down.

"Ouch, right in my ear." Trish rubbed her ringing ear. "Did you have to be so loud?"

"He's just letting 'em all know he's king." Patrick smoothed the already gleaming black shoulder as he unhooked the green web gate across the stall entrance. "Now, you trot once around and then gallop nice and easy another. Let him get the kinks out." Patrick boosted Trish into the saddle. "We'll give him a short work tomorrow."

Trish nodded. She slid her feet into the iron stirrups and clucked her horse forward. Spitfire walked with that loose-limbed gait that told Trish he was completely relaxed. His stride lengthened as they approached the entrance to the track and Trish went to a post as he trotted out to the left.

The soothing rhythm made it too easy for her mind to keep chewing on David's comment. If *he* had a bad feeling—David wasn't one to talk much about his feelings. And for him to—Trish jerked her attention back to the present. She had to concentrate on riding. Accidents happened too easily when a rider let the mind wander.

"Wish I could just keep riding," Trish muttered when she slid to the ground, much too soon for her liking.

While she'd tried to think of answers for her interviewer, Trish knew that journalists often threw a curve.

And that's exactly what he did.

"Where will you be riding after the Belmont?" Bill Williams looked up from his writing pad.

"I—I'm not sure." Trish couldn't think up anything but the truth. "You see, I promised to make up a chemistry class this summer. The school let me drop it when I was having too much trouble with that and racing and all the other stuff going on."

"By other stuff, you mean your father's illness?"

Trish nodded. *Why, oh why, had she mentioned the chemistry?* "Dad and I originally talked about Long Acres in Seattle, but I've been invited to ride in California, too, so—"

"Is chemistry really so important?"

"No, but my promise is." Trish felt a flush start up her neck. *How could she switch the subject?*

"Other young riders get their GED or hire a tutor. Or just drop out of school. What do you think you'll do?"

Trish took a deep breath. "My mom would never let me get my GED or drop out. She thinks college is really important."

"What do *you* think?"

"Well," Trish paused to give her brain time to get in gear before she said something she'd be sorry for. "School is important. But so is racing. Somehow we'll just have to work it all out."

When Williams finally said goodbye, Trish felt like she'd been scrubbed and hung up to dry like the bandages that swung from the wire along the aisle. She left the tack room and slipped under the web gate in Spitfire's stall.

"Come on, you guys, let's eat." She gave Spitfire a quick hug. "I'd rather wash ten horses than go through an interview again."

"You sounded pretty cool to me." David picked up the bucket full of grooming gear. Trish watched as David put all the brushes and cloths away in the tack box. His whistle told her he'd gotten rid of the bad feeling he'd had. She knew where it had gone. Right to the pit of her stomach.

"Hey, what's the matter with our Derby winner?" Red held the door for them as they entered the track kitchen. "You look like you lost your best friend."

I did, Trish almost answered. Her father had flown back home for treatment that morning.

"She just had a go-round with that writer from *Sports Illustrated,*" David answered for her. "She got caught on 'where are you racing after Belmont'?"

"Well?" Red grinned at her. "Where are you?"

"I wish I knew." Trish picked up a tray and set it down hard on the counter. Here she was a Derby winner, and right now she felt about as low as the last-place rider.

Temper, temper. And if there was any way to strangle her resident critic, that would be fine, too.

Trish ignored the three men talking around her as she mixed black cherry yogurt with crunchy, dry cereal. While the combination didn't look the greatest, it tasted good and was good for her. *Why did I bring up the chemistry? Now Mom will feel—who knows what she'll feel? Right now I feel like hiding and bawling for a week or two.* She licked the yogurt off her spoon. She could feel the tears burning the back of her eyelids.

This is stupid. You have nothing to cry about, her little nagger leaped back into the act.

"I'll see you guys back at the barn." Trish picked up her tray and left, ignoring their protests. But no matter how fast she walked, she couldn't get away from the thoughts swirling in her head.

Good Christians don't get down like this. You should be ashamed of yourself. You have so much to be grateful for.

It's okay, buddy, you're just tired. We've been through a lot the last few days. And besides, your dad just left. That's always hard.

Trish decided she liked the second voice better. And it was true. She knew all about adrenalin highs, the kind that carry you through the excitement and then dump you down the next day.

"God, help us," she pleaded as she slipped into Spitfire's stall and sank down in the straw in the corner. "Please take care of my dad—and us." Spitfire snuffled her hair and licked away a tear that had escaped and trickled down her cheek. Trish laid her head on her arms and let the tears roll. Spitfire stood over her, as if keeping guard.

By the time the others returned, slightly red eyes and a wayward sniff or two were the only signs of the storm that had passed.

The sound of laughter drew Trish to the tack room. She leaned against the doorway as Patrick, deep in his story, bent forward to deliver the punch line. Red and David, both with saddlesoaped cloths in their hands, listened and cleaned tack at the same time.

When her chuckle chimed in with the others, Patrick waved Trish to a chair without a break in his monologue. She settled back for a pleasant time. His stories could go on all day and into the night if encouraged.

Two hours later and feeling more like herself, Trish took advantage of a break and stood up. Her sides ached from laughing. The tack room looked like Mr. Clean had just sent his whirlwind through.

"I need to go study for a while. Those finals are coming right up," Trish announced.

"Need some help?" Red looked up with a hopeful grin.

"Thanks, but no thanks. Besides, what do you know about government in Washington state?"

"I could ask you questions."

"Sure," David added. "About racing times and track conditions."

Red snapped a rag at David's knee. "Thanks. You're a big help."

David tossed Trish the car keys. "Pick me up after evening feed."

"I'll bring him back." Red turned his teasing gaze up to Trish. "That way you can study without interruption. Then maybe we can all go to a movie later."

Patrick walked Trish to the car. "Sure you'll be all right now?"

"Thanks for the stories." Trish leaned on the open car door. "You always make me feel better."

"Now, you'd be a-tellin' me if I can help?"

Trish nodded. "Thanks again."

———

Tuesday morning dawned heavily overcast, with predictions of rain. Even the breeze felt wet in her face as Trish galloped Spitfire around the track. While she kept him controlled, he still had a sweat-popping run. As she walked him around to cool him down, Trish thought back to the night before.

The three of them had gone to a movie, and sitting next to Red made her feel warm and restless. Until he took her hand in his—then she just felt warm. A feeling that was just right. David had punched her lightly on the arm on the way out of the theater. Just thinking about it sent a blush to her neck. So far she hadn't seen Red again this morning. How would she act? What should she say?

CHAPTER 3

She didn't have to say or do anything. Trish didn't see Red all Tuesday morning. Or that afternoon.

"And what might be botherin' my girl today?" Patrick asked after lunch at the track kitchen.

"She's in love." David dodged Trish's well-aimed fist. "First love." He ducked again.

Laughter twinkled from Patrick's sky-blue eyes. "And I wouldn't have to be a-askin' who the young man might be."

"I'm not in *love*." Trish ignored the blush she felt creeping up her neck. "I'm in—like."

Patrick and David looked over their shoulders at each other, then fought to keep from exploding.

"If you two can't act any more mature than that, I'll just go on back to the hotel and get to work. *Somebody* has to be an adult around here." Trish rose to her feet, her chin tilted in a determined don't-mess-with-me angle.

"Tricia Evanston?"

Trish stopped before she bumped into the young man she recognized as one of the jockey agents.

"Yes." She set her tray back down on the table.

"My name is Jonathan Smith." He extended his hand. "Do you have a minute?"

Trish nodded as she shook his hand. "Sure. You want to talk here?"

"This will be fine." He nodded as Trish introduced David and Patrick. "Good to see you again, Patrick. Glad to have you back." He settled into the chair on the other side of Trish. "Is it true that you haven't signed with an agent?"

Trish nodded. "I haven't needed to. In Portland I had all the mounts I could handle."

"Well, a trainer came and asked me to get you to ride for him tomorrow afternoon." Smith checked a paper he took from his pocket. "That would be in the third race. Are you interested?"

"Of course." Trish leaned forward. She clenched her fists to keep her hands from clapping.

"You understand that you'll need to sign a contract with me?"

Trish nodded. She had known that one day it would come to this. But she thought she'd have to find an agent herself—not that one would find her. And in Kentucky.

Jonathan pulled a folded paper from his shirt pocket. "It's very simple, really. You can look it over if you like." He handed Trish the typed form.

"I'd like my father to read this, if that's okay." Trish scanned the simple document. Her eyes stopped at the paragraph that detailed the fees. While twenty-five percent was normal, she hated giving the agent that much of her winnings.

"Dad's not here," David reminded her softly.

Trish caught her bottom lip between her teeth. "You need this signed before tomorrow?"

The man nodded.

"One thing you should know. I don't take a jockey fee

when I ride Spitfire, or any of our own horses, for that matter. That means you wouldn't get any money, either."

Jonathan tipped back on the legs of the chair. He crossed his arms over his chest, appearing to be deep in thought. "Usually an agent gets his cut on any ride." He thumped his chair back solidly on the floor. "Let's be honest, Tricia. You are in a strong position to win the Preakness or at least come in the money. That makes you a valuable property, to me or any other agent. And face it, I'm in the business to make money, too. But I can only charge you for the mounts I get for you." A smile worked its way up to his eyes. "One thing I'll make sure of, you'll be racing more and more for farms other than your father's."

Trish handed the contract to David. "What do you think?" she asked as he and Patrick finished reading it.

"It's standard," Patrick replied. "And besides, if he doesn't do a good job for you, you can fire him and hire someone else."

Trish grinned at the twinkle she saw dancing in the old man's eyes. She reached across the table and pulled a pen from David's pocket. After signing her name, she handed the paper back to the agent.

"Thank you." Jonathan refolded the paper and put it back in his pocket. "I'll see if I can get more mounts for you before you leave—Thursday, right?"

Trish nodded. "Early, most likely."

"And you want to ride at Pimlico?" It was more a statement than a question.

Trish nodded again.

"Good. I'll be talking with you." He shook hands with her and the others, and strode out of the room.

Trish settled back against her chair and stretched her

arms above her head. "Well, that's done." Doubts chased each other through her mind like kids playing tag.

"You needn't worry about whether you did the right thing, you know," Patrick said, reading her mind. "As long as you're under age and all."

"He's right," David added. "Dad could cancel the contract if he thought you weren't being treated right."

Trish frowned. "But I gave my word."

"I know," Patrick said. "Just be rememberin' that Jonathan works for *you*. You don't work for him." He pushed his chair back and rose to his feet. "And now, I'll be getting back to our prince, and you can get back to your books. The day'll be gone before we know it."

Returning to the hotel, Trish hit the books with a flourish. She read two chapters for history, then started on *War and Peace* for English. It didn't take long to realize she should have started the book much earlier. She was still trying to figure out who all the characters were when the phone rang.

"Jonathan Smith here," the man responded to her greeting. "I have another mount for you tomorrow, if you'd like it. Seventh race, a claiming for fillies and mares."

"Great—uh, let me check something." Trish shuffled some papers by the phone. "Dad's put in a claim for Sarah's Pride in that race. Will that be a problem?"

"Shouldn't. That's not the horse I have for you. You'll take it then?"

"Yes—and thanks." Trish could feel a smile stretching her cheeks, causing bubbles of happiness to rise and float above her head. As they popped, they showered giggles all over her. *Wait till I tell David—and Red.* When she thought of Red the bubbles bounced higher. *And Dad. If only he were here. I'll have to call him tonight.* Two mounts for Wednesday. In Kentucky—at Churchill Downs. Not bad for a sixteen-year-old kid from Vancouver, Washington—definitely *not* the horse capital of the world.

Trish had a hard time getting back into *War and Peace.*

Good thing I read fast, she thought as she drove to the track to pick up David, *or that book could take a year.* She waved at the guard on the gate and drove back to barn 41. Spitfire nickered as soon as she whistled; a horse on the other side of the barn answered him. David, Red, and Patrick lounged in the tack room.

"How'd you do today?" she asked Rod.

He shook his head. "Good thing they pay something for those of us who don't come in the money. Otherwise my bank account would be in reverse."

"Like that nag you had in the last race?" David asked as he stretched his hands above his head.

"You gotta understand, boy," Patrick got in his digs, "that horse couldn't even go backwards—it just quit."

Trish grinned at the teasing. It was nice not to be the brunt of it for a change. "What races are you in tomorrow?"

Red squinted his eyes, trying to remember. "Think I have three so far. First, fifth, and seventh." He nodded. "Yeah, that's right."

"Shame you're not up in the third. Then I could beat you in two races."

Red thumped his chair back on all four legs. "You got another mount? Way to go! That calls for a celebration! Come on, I'm buying you a super-size Diet Coke. You two wanna join us?" He threw an arm around Trish's shoulders and waited for an answer.

Patrick and David looked at each other and shrugged, slowly pulling themselves up from their chairs.

"You're sure we won't be in the way?" Patrick's face looked uncharacteristically innocent—almost cherubic.

Trish felt like stomping on his foot, but the weight of Red's arm seemed to lock her jaw and her feet. He tugged her around, and she kept pace with the three of them as they walked to the car.

They ordered dinner, and the time passed in a haze of laughter. Patrick topped every story anyone started. The waitress must have thought they were high on something. They were—on happiness.

That night Trish called Rhonda. She broke out in giggles as she told her about Red.

"You really like him, don't you?"

"I guess so. Remember your teasing me about Doug Ramstead last fall?" Trish twirled her hair around a finger. "And I never even got to go out with him."

"Yeah. He's still a hunk, too."

"Well, Red's *here*. Wish you could meet him. He and David pick on me about as much as Brad and David did, but it's different. Really different."

"I miss you," Rhonda wailed.

"Yeah, me too. David's flying home for Brad's graduation. Wish I could. Just think, one more of our musketeers is done with Prairie High. Only you and I'll be left."

"Yeah. And you're never here."

When Trish hung up half an hour later, she winced at the thought of the phone bill. Talking from halfway across the country wasn't the same as a mile away. She lay back on her bed and thought of all the news Rhonda had told her about school. If only Rhonda could come to Kentucky. It seemed as if school and Vancouver were in another life. *Distance does that,* she remembered her father saying.

Thinking about him made Trish jerk upright and dial Runnin' On Farm. There was no answer. She checked her watch. Nine o'clock central time meant seven at home.

"David." She stood and walked into the living room where he was watching television. "There's no answer at home. Where do you think Mom and Dad are?" A frown wrinkled her forehead.

David blinked awake and rubbed his eyes. A yawn caught him before he could answer. He checked his watch. Seeing the time brought him instantly awake.

"You suppose they're at the hospital?" He ran a hand through the dark curls that fell on his forehead.

Trish walked across the room to the window and stared out, her teeth tugging her bottom lip. "David, remember that bad feeling you had? Well, I've got it now."

CHAPTER 4

Trish awoke to the phone ringing on Wednesday morning. Her heart seemed to leap right out of her chest. She fumbled for both the phone and the lamp switch. *What's wrong with Spitfire?* chased *Could it be Dad?* through her brain.

"Hello?" Even her voice sounded scared.

"Good morning, Tee."

Trish collapsed back against the pillows. "Hi, Mom. What's wrong?"

"We just wanted to get in touch with you two before you left for the track. Sorry to call so early."

"That's okay." Trish leaned over to shut off the alarm. "It was time to get up anyway. How's Dad?"

"Not doing real well right now. He had a bad reaction to the chemo and the doctor wants to do more tests."

"More tests?"

"It's routine at this point, and they may have to change his medication. Anyway, we won't be flying back today as we'd planned. Dad says he'll call you this evening and let you know whether to go on without us or not."

Trish felt as if she'd been punched in the gut. "But—but . . . Is Dad there? Can I talk with him?"

"He's at the hospital now, and finally sleeping. He

34

was up and down all night. I just came home to check on things here and pick up some clean clothes." Marge's voice had an edge of worry to it again. She took a deep breath. "How are things going there?"

For an instant Trish couldn't even remember why she'd tried to call the night before. "We called last night. I knew something was wrong when no one answered." She paused for her thoughts to catch up with her. "Tell Dad I signed with an agent. I have two mounts this afternoon."

"Are you sure that's the best thing to do? You know you'll be heading back to school as soon as Belmont is over." Her mother's worry was more obvious now.

"Mo-om."

"I'm sorry, Trish. I can't even think straight right now. Just be careful. Tell David we'll talk to him tonight. Goodbye now."

Trish stared at the phone in her hand. *If only I could have talked with Dad.* She could feel the tears prick at the back of her eyes.

Don't be such a baby, her little nagger scolded. *He was at the hospital, not the farm. You know, if you'd pray more . . .* Trish slammed the receiver down. She felt like slamming something else.

She stomped into the other room. "David." She shook his shoulder. "David, how could you sleep through the phone and everything?"

David pulled a pillow over his head, then flipped over with a suddenly wide-awake glare. "What do you mean, the phone?"

"Mom called. They're not coming today and maybe not even tomorrow."

"Dad's worse?" He was really awake now.

"I don't know how bad. He's in the hospital. More tests." Trish balled a section of her nightshirt in her fist. "What do we do now?" she pleaded.

"We take care of Spitfire. Then you study, and ride this afternoon." David reached for his jeans draped across the bottom of his bed. "And we pray like crazy. Now get going. We leave in ten minutes."

Trish wanted to argue—or smack him for his methodical tone. Better yet, she felt like locking herself in the bathroom and turning on the shower so no one could hear her scream.

Instead, she dragged herself back to her room and started dressing. *God, what are you doing with my dad? Why can't things get better instead of worse? Why don't you just leave us alone?*

David and Trish hardly talked on the way to the track. Patrick had Spitfire fed and groomed by the time they arrived.

"Sorry we're late," David said. "Things aren't good at home."

That's the understatement of the year, Trish thought as she leaned against Spitfire's shoulder and rubbed his neck. The colt snuffled her hair and whiskered her cheek as if to cheer her up.

"They know, lass," Patrick said softly behind her. "Animals always know when those they love are hurtin'."

Trish felt the tears again. She buried her face in Spitfire's mane. "Dad's got to get better again. We need him here. I need him. I—" She sniffed back the tears. "Patrick, do you pray?"

"Of course, lass. How else could I be livin' and workin' again? Only God could cure a drunk like me." He swiped a finger across his eyes. "And your father now—

He gave me this job. And I'm thinkin' it's to be takin' care of more than a horse. I'd like to give back some of what your father gave me."

Trish turned and let the old trainer put his arms around her. He patted her back, all the while crooning to her as he did with Spitfire. The music worked the same magic on humans as it did on horses.

Trish mopped her eyes again. "Well, let's get this kid out on the track." She nodded at Spitfire, who pricked his ears at David's tuneless whistle in the aisle. "Thanks, Patrick."

"Your dad'll be here soon." Patrick patted Trish's shoulder. "I feel it in my bones."

"You okay?" David asked when he gave her a leg up. Concern darkened his eyes.

Trish nodded. "We'll make it." She gathered her reins and clucked Spitfire forward.

You know, if you were really a good Christian, you wouldn't worry about your dad like this, her nagger gloated. *And what happened to the old I-will-not-cry Trish?*

God loves you no matter what, her other little voice responded. *Remember, He knows what He's doing now just like He has in the past. Remember when you fell apart in the parking lot at Portland Meadows? God'll take care of you now, too.*

Trish shut both voices off by shoving her boots into the iron stirrups and nudging Spitfire into a trot. But it sure was nice to know *someone* was on her side.

Red saluted her with his whip as he slow-galloped a bay around the track. "See you later?" His question floated back on the slight breeze.

Now that Spitfire was warmed up, Trish turned the

colt clockwise and gave him enough rein for a steady gallop. Spitfire pulled at the restraint, pleading for a chance to run. Trish only laughed at him when he tossed his head at her refusal.

"You big goof. You think you can run anytime you want." She rode high in the stirrups, her weight helping to keep the horse under control. "I should be working those two I'm riding today."

Spitfire flicked his ears back and forth, listening to her voice while keeping track of everything around him.

"You know, if you'd just let someone else ride you like this in the morning, I could go home for Brad's graduation," Trish spoke to the horse. "I might as well be tied in the stall with you."

The colt snorted, shaking his head as if he disagreed with her.

Trish felt as if someone had smacked her between the shoulder blades. What had she just said?

Her nagger didn't miss a beat. *Sure. Here you are doing what every jockey dreams of, and you're griping. There's just no pleasing you, is there? Where's that attitude of gratitude you're supposed to have, anyway?*

"Sorry, fella," Trish muttered to her horse. "It's not your fault we let you get used to only me for a rider." She shrugged off the negative feelings and concentrated on the remaining ride. When she pulled Spitfire back down to a trot, he hadn't run enough to work up a decent sweat.

"You sure are in good condition," Trish told him as they trotted out the track entrance. "I should be running a track myself." Spitfire nodded his agreement. "What do you know about it?" Trish laughed as she jumped to the ground, giving him a playful scratch under his forelock.

"I've gotta go meet my horses and trainers for this afternoon," Trish said after giving Spitfire a last pat. "So don't wait breakfast for me. I'll have to leave for the hotel right after."

Trish checked the barn numbers that her agent Jonathan had written down for her. Numbers 20 and 22—both of them housed the horses of smaller farms.

"Mr. Danielson around?" she asked a young Hispanic man grooming a horse.

"Sí, él está ahí." He pointed to the office as he spoke.

Trish listened hard as her brain translated the words. She smiled back at him. "Gracias." She'd probably do better in Spanish if she'd just make a point of talking to the people around the track. *If they'd only speak slower.*

When Trish approached the office she could hear two men arguing inside.

"But you don't know anything about her," one said.

"She won the Derby, didn't she?" answered the other. "That's enough for me."

"She only won because she was riding her father's colt. No one else would let her near their horses."

Trish felt her ears burning. The flush crept all the way up her face. She walked back outside the barn and leaned against the wall. *Guess I'll just have to prove that I can ride,* she thought. She pushed the hurt she felt down where she couldn't feel it, at least for the moment.

In a few seconds a man wearing a brown sweater strode out of the barn, and the voice of the one who questioned her ability spoke to one of the grooms. Taking a deep breath and pasting a smile on her face, Trish walked back into the barn.

"Mr. Danielson?" She cleared her throat. "I'm Tricia Evanston."

Danielson glanced from Trish to the back of the man striding across the hot-walking area.

Trish lifted her chin to boost her confidence. No matter what anyone thought, she wasn't going to back down on her commitment.

The man nodded slightly as if reading her mind. Then he smiled and extended his hand. "Glad to meet you, Tricia. How about taking this fellow out for a warm-up? Juan, saddle Jiminy for her, please."

The dark bay horse sported a white star between his eyes. Instead of looking friendly and curious like most horses did, he laid his ears back and reached out as if to take a nip.

Trish stopped and studied the animal. "Is he nasty mean or just a tease?"

Danielson grabbed the halter and rubbed the horse's cheek. "Jiminy here is nothing but a big bluff. He thinks he's tough, but—"

"He's really a big softy," Trish finished for him. She extended her palm with a piece of carrot in it. "We have one like him at home, but you have to watch out, because he'll *really* nip you." Trish reached up to scratch the horse's ears and under the short mane.

"He's been in the money twice but never won," Danielson filled her in on the horse's history. "Then he pulled a muscle, and is just coming back." By this time the horse was saddled and Danielson gave Trish a leg up. "Take him half a circuit at a walk and then jog the rest."

Trish kept up her usual stream of sing-song chatter as they circled the track, and Jiminy settled into a ground-eating stride when she turned him to the left. He watched all the action around them as though a spectator instead of a participant. When Trish nudged him to a trot, he settled easily into the gait.

"We're gonna have to light a fire under you, old man," Trish muttered as she rode back to the barn. "I'll see you this afternoon." She slipped Jiminy another carrot chunk as soon as the groom removed the bridle.

"That's a good way to make him your slave for life." Danielson tipped his hat back, then ran a hand down the gelding's shoulder and right foreleg. "Okay, take him away." A woman took the lead and led the horse off to the hot-walker.

"I need to meet another trainer," Trish said as she and Danielson walked back to the office. "So if there's nothing else, I'll see you in the saddling paddock, third race."

"Fine. And by the way, Tricia, don't let some things you might hear get to you." The twinkle in the man's deep blue eyes told Trish he knew she'd overheard the earlier conversation.

Trish grinned back. "Thanks."

She located the next trainer leaning on the fence watching the action on the track. By the time they'd met and talked, it was eight o'clock. His mare had been warmed up earlier. Trish checked her watch. She didn't have a lot of time before she had to be back in the jockey room.

Praying on her way back to the hotel, Trish stopped to catch a fast-food breakfast, knowing the buffet at the hotel would be closed by now. "God, please help me to keep my mind on my work," she prayed aloud, in case God could hear better that way.

In her room she reviewed the characters in *War and Peace* and read further. "These Russian names are gonna do me in," she muttered. "How will I ever write a book report? I can't pronounce the names, let alone spell them."

When it was time to leave for the track, she stuffed the novel and her history book into her sports bag. She could resume study in the jockey room. On the drive out she tried to concentrate on getting geared up for the race. When thoughts of her father intruded, she gritted her teeth and did what he'd always told her to do: *Stick in a Bible verse so the fear can't take over.* Finally, she resorted to a song. "He will raise you up on eagle's wings, bear you . . ." Boy, did she ever need those eagle's wings once again.

"Tricia, there's a red-headed young man out here asking for you." Frances Brown, keeper of the women's jockey room, leaned against the door frame. Trish was camped on one of the beds, making it a study hall. "He seems to have a special interest in you."

Trish couldn't help but respond to the grin that crinkled Frances' face clear up to her eyes. At the thought of Red, a fuzzy feeling warmed Trish's middle. She marked her place in her history book and leaped off the bed. So much for good intentions to study.

"Hi, Trish—got time for a quick soda?" Red greeted her in one breath.

"Sure." Trish smiled back at him. When they bumped shoulders walking into the rec room, she thought back to the time Red had held her hand at the movie. Would he hold it again? The thought sent a familiar flush up her neck. If only she didn't blush so easily.

As soon as they took their sodas to a table and sat down, a couple of other jockeys joined them. It wasn't long before Red was the center of the group. He seemed to draw attention wherever he went. Trish hid her smile behind her paper cup. It felt good to know he had come especially for her.

When Trish followed the other jockeys down the stairs and out to the saddling paddock for the third race, she felt the old familiar butterflies take a couple of practice leaps before beginning their regular show. By the time she fell into step with the trainer Danielson, they were in rare form. Trish swallowed hard. *Settle down.*

"Now, you can use that whip to keep old Jiminy's mind on his business," Danielson said as he gave Trish a leg up. "I like my horses to come from behind, but take advantage of that number two position. Don't let him drift out."

Trish nodded, stuffing her reluctance to use a whip back where it belonged. All horses weren't trained like those at Runnin' On Farm.

Jiminy behaved like a veteran as he galloped out to the starting gate and walked in flat-footed. Trish tightened the reins, forcing him to center his weight on his haunches and prepare for the start.

As the gate clanged open, Jiminy leaped forward in perfect time. Ears pricked, he suddenly seemed to realize what he was supposed to be doing—racing.

"Yeah, that's the way!" Trish shouted at him as they surged past the number one horse and took the rail. "Come on, come on, don't be lazy now." She kept a firm hold on his mouth so he couldn't drift and bump into another horse. With only six furlongs to run, they couldn't miss a beat.

Jiminy held his number one position through the turn and into the final stretch. When two other horses pulled up even with them, Trish went to the whip. Jiminy flattened his black ears and obeyed quickly. His stride lengthened, while heavy grunts matched the pounding of his feet.

One horse kept the pace and began to pull ahead.

Trish encouraged Jiminy again with her voice and the leather whip. Each stride brought the white columns closer. One more command screamed at the twitching ears and they flashed across the wire. They'd won by a nose.

That'll show 'em, Trish thought as she accepted congratulations from the trainer and the owner. She recognized the owner as the man in the brown sweater that morning, the one who'd said she couldn't ride anything but Spitfire.

She smiled for the cameras. This photo would go in a frame on her wall.

When she pulled a fourth place out of a field of ten in the seventh race, Trish didn't feel too badly. The mare she rode tried to quit in the stretch but Trish had kept her running. That in itself was something to be proud of. She had shown her skill as a jockey again.

Besides, Sarah's Pride, the filly her father had put claiming money on, had won. Runnin' On Farm now owned a new horse. Trish followed David and Patrick as they led their new acquisition back to the barn.

"Ya done good, lass," Patrick said. "Guess that'll show 'em what you're made of."

Trish grinned. "Feels good."

When they got back to the hotel that evening, the message light was flashing on their phone.

"Sorry, kids," Hal's voice sounded both sad and weak when they returned his call. "I just won't make it in time. You'll have to go on to Pimlico without me."

CHAPTER 5

"But Dad, what's wrong? Why can't you come now?"

"Trish—"

"Are you sicker and not telling us?" Trish could hardly keep the tears from choking her voice.

"Tee, listen to me. I don't want to talk about this over the phone. All the arrangements for your trip are in place and Mom and I'll just be a bit later, that's all. Besides, this way I won't have to make that long drive. We'll fly directly to Baltimore."

"I guess."

"Now, is David there? Put him on the other phone."

"I'm here, Dad. Have been all along."

Hal finished giving them directions to the Crosskeys Inn and on how to manage the trip. "You'll meet Mel Howell at Pimlico. I've already talked with him. Oh, and Trish?"

"Yeah."

"I think you should ride in the van just in case the horses need you. I love you kids more than you'll ever know."

After they said goodbye, Trish returned the receiver to its cradle and sprawled spread-eagle across her bed. Nothing was turning out as it was supposed to. Her father had been getting better before they started traveling. Maybe they shouldn't have come to Kentucky. Would staying home have helped? Maybe her mother had been right all along.

Later that night Trish couldn't get comfortable in bed. She turned one way and then the other. She punched the pillows up and kicked the bedspread off. Kicking felt good. *If only there were some way to kick the cancer.* Finally she turned the light back on, propped herself up on two pillows and reached for the carved eagle her father had placed on her nightstand before he left. She smoothed a finger over the perfectly carved feathers. "If only we could soar like you," she whispered.

Placing the figure back under the light, Trish picked up her Bible. The verse in Isaiah 40 hadn't changed, but the first words caught her attention. "They that wait upon the Lord . . ." She read them again. Waiting had never been one of her favorite pastimes.

Her father was learning to wait. He'd said so.

She'd rather have the eagle's wings *now.* She read the rest of the verse. ". . . shall run and not be weary; they shall walk and not faint." Boy, did she need these promises now. She shut the book and closed her eyes. The words to pray wouldn't come, only a picture of an eagle catching the thermals and soaring above the cliffs.

Finally, Trish snapped off the light and burrowed under the covers. "Thank you, God—I think. Please take care of my dad." The next thing she knew the alarm was ringing.

Dawn had pinked the sky by the time Trish and David drove through the gates at Churchill Downs. They'd taken the time to pack up and check out of the hotel.

At the stall both horses were still eating. Trish told Patrick what her father had said, then opened the tack boxes to begin packing for the trip. Everything was in order—ropes wound neatly, buckets stacked. Even the feed sacks were tied off.

"Patrick, you're super." Trish turned and smiled her appreciation. "Thank you."

"David and I did that yesterday, figuring we'd be leaving early. All that's left is the stuff from this morning." Patrick tipped his fedora back and scratched his forehead. "I'm all packed too, so after you loosen 'em up, we'll be ready to load."

Trish felt herself saying goodbye to Churchill Downs as she trotted Spitfire around the track. It wasn't like at home where she knew she'd be back in the fall. After all, how many times did a West Coast farm get to bring a horse to the Derby?

"Maybe I'll ride here sometime on my own. What do you think?" Spitfire twitched his ears and shook his head. "Thanks for the vote of confidence." She patted his neck and tightened him down to a walk. "Maybe we'll get to bring you here for the Breeder's Cup in October. What would you think of that?" Spitfire snorted. "Was that a yes or a no?" The black colt tugged on the bit and pranced sideways as they left the track. "See if I ask your opinion again." Trish jumped to the ground and handed the reins over to Patrick. She gave Spitfire a quick scratch while David switched the saddle to Sarah's Pride.

"How's our girl this morning?" Trish spoke softly to the bright-sorrel filly. With one hand clamped on the reins under the filly's chin, Trish used the other to work magic around the horse's ears and down her cheek. Sarah's Pride pricked her ears and nosed Trish's shoulder. She dropped her head lower to make it easier for

Trish to reach under the bridle behind her ears. Trish smoothed the forelock and rubbed down the horse's neck.

"You'll be puttin' her to sleep that way," Patrick said as he watched Trish get better acquainted.

"Well, we better not do that." Trish raised her knee, and with David's assistance swung smoothly into the saddle. "Come on, girl, let's see how you behave."

Sarah's Pride wanted to run. She snorted and pranced, throwing in a bounce or two to keep Trish alert. Halfway around the first turn, the filly shied at a blowing paper. A few strides farther she stopped to stare at something only she could see.

By the time they returned to the barn, Trish felt as if she'd been working Gatesby, the horse who gave her so much trouble at home.

"No wonder she doesn't usually win," Trish said as she slid to the ground. "She can't keep her mind on what she's doing. If she races like she works—" Trish shook her head. "And look at her, she's lathered from just that bit we did. My girl, even I know you've got some conditioning ahead of you." Trish slipped the filly a carrot piece.

"Never mind, lass. We'll turn her into a racehorse yet." Patrick stripped off the tack while David brought out the wash gear. Once the filly was washed down and scraped dry, Trish took the lead.

"I'll walk her. Then let's eat. That truck'll be here anytime."

Red fell into step beside Trish after a couple of rounds on the sanded walking circle. "Hi. Guess you're leaving pretty soon, huh?"

"Yeah. Dad's meeting us in Baltimore."

"Um-m-m." Red seemed uncomfortable. "I'll be back in a minute."

Trish watched him trot back to their stalls. "What's the matter with him?" The filly kept on walking.

"Here, let me finish." David reached for the lead shank as soon as he joined her.

"What's up?" She looked from her brother to Red.

"I need to talk with you a minute." Red nodded toward the grassy area behind the barns. "How about over there?"

"Fine, I guess." She looked at David, who just shrugged. "But I don't have much time."

"You rode really well yesterday." Red kicked a stone in front of them.

"Thanks." Trish's shoulder felt warm where it rubbed against his. If only he'd take her hand again. If only she were brave enough to take his.

Red kicked the stone again. It skittered across the gravel. Sounds from the barns faded into the distance.

"I—I'm really going to miss you." Red turned to Trish, and they stopped under a spreading oak tree. "I have something for you—to remember me by. But I'll see you again."

Trish swallowed against the tight knot in her throat. She drew circles in the dewy grass with the toe of her boot.

"Here." Red took her hand in his and placed a small box in it.

The knot turned into a lump in Trish's throat that threatened to choke her.

"Open it." Red leaned closer.

Trish smoothed the blue velvet of the flat box, and finally opened it. She gasped at the sight of a finely

etched gold cross on a delicate chain. "Oh, Red, it's beautiful!" Her smile trembled, threatening tears.

"You like it then?"

"Oh, yes." Trish lifted the cross and draped the chain
across her palm.

"Here, let me put it on for you." Red took it from her,
looped the chain around her neck, and fastened the
clasp. "Now you have something to remember me by."
He turned her to face him again and placed his lips on
hers. It was a first kiss—tentative and sweet.

"Thank you—for the cross," Trish whispered as she
stepped back. "But I didn't need anything to remind me
of you."

Red smiled. "I'll see you at Belmont for sure, Pimlico
if I can possibly make it." He brushed a lock of hair from
her cheek. "I want to be there when you take the Triple
Crown."

Trish nodded, but couldn't speak. Her voice was lost
somewhere in the sadness of leaving.

Red threaded his fingers through hers, and they am-
bled back to the barn.

———————

Trish wiped the tears from her cheeks as they drove
out the gates of Churchill Downs. She waved to Red once
more, and settled back for the trip. Everything had con-
spired to speed them on their way, and the horses had
loaded as if they were looking forward to a new place.
There hadn't been a line in the Track Kitchen, and the
truck had arrived early.

Trish had been pleasantly surprised when the truck
drove up. Fred Robertson, the driver who had taken
them in from the airport, had requested the trip.

The drive was long but uneventful. Trish checked on the horses when they stopped for lunch. Spitfire nickered when he heard her voice and snuffled her hair as she checked the tie ropes and water buckets.

After lunch Trish slept for a couple of hours. It kept her from thinking about having left Red and about the fact that her father was not with them. It was a good thing Fred had lots of stories to tell about racing and about the country they were passing through. His company helped Trish through her sadness.

They pulled up to the gate at Pimlico at seven o'clock. Racing was over for the day and the evening chores finished. The area was quiet. Trish stifled a feeling of disappointment as she compared the old track at Pimlico to Churchill Downs.

Fred read her feelings and said, "Not to worry. This place may not be as fancy as the Downs, but wait till you see how they treat you here. You and that black colt of yours are stars now, and Mel will take good care of you."

"Mel?"

"Here he comes now. Mel Howell is Chief of Security for the Maryland Racing Association. He has a headful of tales you won't believe."

Trish watched the man with military bearing approach them. His smile erased any stiffness as he stuck his hand in the truck window to shake hands with Robertson.

"Good to see you, you old horse hauler. Been some time since you made it all the way to Baltimore."

"Ah know. But ah brought you someone mahghty special. Tricia Evanston, meet Mel Howell. That's her brother and trainer in the car behind us."

"Welcome, Tricia. I've been looking forward to meeting the young lady who's set everyone on their ears. I hear you won yesterday, too."

Trish felt as if she'd just met an old friend. "Thank you. It's hard to believe I'm really here."

"Well, let's get you settled. Spitfire's stall is all ready. Fred, you know the way to the Stakes barn. I'll ride in the car so I can meet the others."

Robertson eased the van through the gate and past several barns that glowed a faded rose in the evening light. The Stakes barn was last, at the northernmost corner of the back side. It sported a fresh coat of tan paint with white trim. Potted shrubs and freshly raked sand aisles set the Stakes barn apart from the gentle decay of the other barns.

As soon as the truck stopped, Trish leaped down from the cab and swung open the doors to the van. Spitfire nickered and tossed his head. Sarah's Pride turned her head as far as the tie-downs allowed and joined the greeting.

"You two ready to go for a walk?" Trish asked as she palmed a piece of carrot for each. "Bet you're hungry, too." As soon as she heard the ramp clang into position, she slipped the knot on Spitfire's lead and led him toward the door. She started down the ramp but Spitfire paused in the opening. His challenging whinny floated on the evening air. Horses answered from barns on two sides of them. He trumpeted again, pawing the straw in the truck with one front hoof.

"Show off." Trish tugged on the lead. Spitfire shook himself, then followed her down the padded ramp, his hooves thudding a rhythm that hinted at excitement.

"Yours is stall number ten. We left it in sand like your

father requested, and there's plenty of straw in place. We've put your filly in the barn there." Mel pointed to the barn that nearly formed a T with the Stakes barn, except for the drive between them. He turned to Patrick. "Sure is good to see you back in the business. We saved you a spot upstairs in the same barn, if that's okay."

"Good to be back." Patrick tipped his hat off his forehead. "Looks like most of your boarders are already here." He gestured to the horses that watched out their stall doors.

"Only two more after you. The guards are all in place. You can sleep easy tonight."

Trish kept an ear on their conversation and an eye on the trailer where Sarah's Pride had joined David at the doorway. Like Spitfire, she announced her arrival and waited for the responses. Then she danced down the incline like a little girl let out to play.

Trish and David walked the two horses around the Stakes barn several times while Patrick oversaw the tack box moving and prepared the evening feed.

Fred waited until they had the horses bedded down and had hauled Patrick's suitcases up to his room. He shook hands all around and stopped at Trish.

"Ah'll be praying for you," he said softly, "and yuh daddy. It's been mah privilege to be your driver."

Trish started to shake his hand but instead threw her arms around his neck and hugged him. "Thank you. You made both our drives a lot of fun—and I even learned something. Lots of things, in fact." She stepped back in time to see a tear brighten his eyes. "Wish you could stay for the next trip."

"Me, too." He pulled his hat on his head. "Y'all take care now." With a final wave he climbed back into his truck and drove off.

Trish watched until the taillights cleared the gate. She seemed to be saying an awful lot of goodbyes lately.

As the truck drove out, a long white limo pulled in and drove right up to the barn. A uniformed man stepped out.

"I'd like you to meet your personal driver for the time you're at Pimlico," Mel said. "Trish and David Evanston, this is Hank Benson. Hank is a police officer here and volunteers to drive on his off hours."

Trish felt her jaw drop open and hang suspended. *A limo—and driver—for us?* She turned to David. He was trying to remain cool. He kept his jaw in place, but he couldn't talk either.

"Well, that's a first." Patrick shook his head. "Ya been flumoxed, I'd say. Downright flumoxed."

Trish forced her eyes off the limo and asked, "Flumoxed? Patrick, you made that word up."

"Me?" Patrick had his most-innocent look firmly in place—if the laughter shaking his shoulders didn't dislodge it. "You know, lass, pole-axed." At her look of total confusion, he turned to Mel for help.

"Surprised. Shocked." Mel pushed his white Pimlico hat back on his head and shrugged.

"Right." Trish shook her head. Adults didn't always make sense.

"I'm pleased to meet all of you." Hank Benson smiled around the circle. "Now, if you'd like, I'll put your suitcases in the trunk."

"You can leave your car here," Mel told David. "Just take your gear and lock it up. No one will bother it."

While David went to get their suitcases, Mel said, "I'll be around after morning works to take you and David on a tour of Pimlico. If you have any questions, we can answer them for you then. There's a good restaurant at the Crosskeys, and of course a kitchen here at the track for the morning."

Trish couldn't keep from giggling as she settled against the soft leather seat in the limo. Her fingers itched to push all the buttons on the panel to see what they were for. The TV was obvious. There was also a stereo, and a mini-refrigerator stocked with soft drinks and ice.

"Trish, knock it off," David hissed. "You're as bad as a little kid." His fingers ignored his own words and pressed a button that rolled down the window between them and the driver.

"Anything I can help you with?" Benson's voice sounded metallic over the intercom. "Help yourselves to drinks and snacks. Glasses are behind that sliding panel if you'd like ice."

Trish melted back against the seat after fixing her Diet Coke. "Now *this* is the life."

Hank Benson clicked the intercom back on. "We've been following your career, Trish. My daughter, Genny, thinks the sun rises and sets on you."

"How old is she?" Trish tried to rest her glass casually on the leather arm beside her.

"Twelve, and horse-crazy is far too weak a description of her. Says she's going to be a jockey just like you. Maybe sometime while you're here she can meet you."

"Sure. Would she like to meet Spitfire too?"

"Do kids like ice cream?" Hank chuckled. "She has pictures of the two of you on her bedroom walls." He swung the long vehicle into an underground parking garage and stopped in front of the glass doors marked EN-TRANCE. "Now let's get you settled. What time would you like me to pick you up in the morning?"

"Would five be okay?" David suggested.

"You know, you can sleep in a bit if you want. Morning works last until 9:30." Hank slid out of the driver's side and came around to open the passenger door. "Might as well take it easy while you can. Besides, the reporters will mob you once you're at the track."

Trish felt her butterflies take a dive. She still didn't feel comfortable talking to the press. *What if I sound like an idiot?* "Six would be great."

The bellboy showed them to connecting rooms. "You can still order from room service," he said, "but the dining room is about to close."

David thanked him, even remembering to give him a tip. He handed Trish a menu and studied one himself. As soon as they'd called in their order, Trish dialed Runnin' On Farm to let her parents know they'd arrived safely.

There was no answer.

CHAPTER 6

"Try the hospital," David said.

"I thought sure they'd be home by now." Trish ran her hand through her bangs.

"I know, but try." David dug in his billfold for the number. "Here."

Trish breathed a sigh of relief when Marge answered the phone to Hal's hospital room. "Hi, Mom. What's happening?"

"You guys made it okay?"

"Sure. How's Dad?" Trish held the phone away from her ear so David could hear, too.

"He's better tonight. Here, you can talk with him."

Trish held the receiver so hard her fingers cramped. "Hi, Dad. We miss you." She tried to swallow the gravel in her throat so her voice would sound normal.

"Hi, Tee. I miss you guys, too. Is David there?" Hal's voice sounded faint, as if he were far away from the phone.

"Right here." David cleared his throat.

"Now I don't want you to worry, but we won't be coming until Saturday. We should have test results back tomorrow and then we can leave. Mom's booked the tickets for Saturday morning."

"You sure you're not holding out on us?" Trish couldn't keep her tone light. While her father sounded calm, something inside her felt like screaming.

"We'll talk about all that's happened when we get there. Both horses shipped okay?"

"Yeah, and settled in fine." David tilted the receiver so he could talk easier. "Patrick is great. We couldn't do it without him."

"Wait till you meet Mel Howell," Trish added. She couldn't just listen, she had so much to tell her dad. "Oh, and wait till you see our limo! David and I almost got lost in it." She felt her butterflies leap for joy when her father chuckled softly.

Trish hadn't begun to touch on all she wanted to say before her father said he'd see them Saturday and hung up. She sank down on the edge of the bed.

"Did he sound weaker, or am I just making things up?"

David started clipping his nails. The clicking sound was distracting and annoyed Trish.

"David!"

He took a deep breath and looked up to meet Trish's stare. "Yes. And no, you're not making things up. I'll—" A knock on the door interrupted him. "There's our dinner."

Trish felt her stomach rumble as a waiter rolled in a white cloth-covered table. Silver domes covered the plates and a trio of yellow daisies bobbed in a bud vase. Even their Diet Cokes were served in crystal goblets.

When the waiter raised the domes, Trish snickered at the cheeseburgers and fries. They should have ordered steak or chicken. The table was much too fancy for burgers.

David tipped the waiter and sank into a chair. "I can't decide if I'm just beat, or really starved." He offered Trish the ketchup first, then doused his fries with it. "I should have ordered a chocolate shake. We earned a treat today."

———————

Later, in bed, Trish flicked off the lamp. Light from an outside spotlight outlined her window where she hadn't pulled the drape all the way shut. At home the yardlight always cast friendly shadows into her room. Vancouver seemed so far away. About as far away as God right now.

In the morning reporters were waiting for Trish. When Hank eased the limo to a stop, she noticed a woman with a tape recorder, and a man leaning against the Stakes barn wall with a camera slung around his neck. They seemed to be together.

Trish wished she could slip down and disappear through the cracks in the seat. Maybe she could make a quick exit out the opposite side of the car and go directly to Spitfire's stall.

Reading her thoughts, David jabbed her with his elbow. "Come on, chicken liver. You'll do fine."

Easy for you to say, Trish thought. *You're not the one to look like an idiot if you say the wrong thing.* She took a deep breath and followed David out the open door. Hank Benson winked at her, giving her the high sign with his thumb on the door.

Trish pasted a smile on her face. She could hear her father's voice in her ear: *Smiling makes you feel better about yourself, even if you don't feel like it. And it always makes other people think better of you.* So keep on smiling, she ordered her face. *And knock it off,* she commanded her inner aerial troop. *You can do your acrobatics later.*

"Good morning, what can I do for you?" she heard herself say.

That's the way, girl, her inner voice cheered her on. For a change, the nagging twin must have been sleeping.

"Just a few questions," the female journalist said. She clicked on the recorder. "You don't mind, do you?" She nodded at her equipment. When Trish shook her head, the woman continued. "How does it feel to be the first female to win the Kentucky Derby?"

"Probably the same as the guys feel. Happy, excited, like a dream come true. Most of them have worked longer for it than I have. So I guess that makes me appreciate the honor even more."

"They say the only reason you won is because you were on your father's horse."

Trish could feel the hair bristling on the back of her neck. "I know that's what some people are saying, but I helped raise that horse and I trained him, with my dad's instructions. We're a team, all of our family." She unclenched her fists. "And I've won a lot of races when I wasn't riding Spitfire, even in Kentucky."

"I hear your father is very sick. What will you do if he can't make the trip?"

Trish gritted her teeth. A quick *Father, help!* winged skyward as she scrambled for an answer. "Then Spitfire and I will race like my dad taught us. You can't do more than your best. And we don't do less."

Trish glanced up to see David's arm raised in victory. The approval made her bolder. "You see, we believe God is with us and guides us, around a racetrack, or . . ." She took another deep breath and lifted her chin a fraction. ". . . in a hospital."

The reporter seemed at a loss for words. "Why—uh—

thank you, Tricia. I'm sure you have plenty of work to do this morning. And good luck here at Pimlico." She put her microphone away and gestured to the cameraman to follow her.

Luck, schmuck. Trish kept the words inside while her smile stayed in place. "It was nice meeting you." Feeling as if she had the last word, Trish stuffed her hands in her pockets and went in search of Patrick.

"I tried." Trish plunked down on a bale of hay in the tack room.

"I'm sure you did fine. Ya needn't be worryin' yerself." Patrick's brogue always thickened when he felt deeply about something. "Besides, most o' the time, them reporters don't get half what you say. Get yerself up there on that colt. You'll feel better."

"You're right." Trish nodded, slapped her hands on her knees, and nodded again. "At least Spitfire doesn't ask questions."

The dirt road to the track seemed long as Trish and Spitfire passed by the rows of barns. While the buildings seemed shabby, the morning orchestra was the same as on tracks everywhere—metal jangling, horses snorting and nickering, stable folk laughing, a shout or whistle thrown in for counterpoint. It was comfortable music, the kind that Trish planned always to be a part of.

When they turned left on the track, Spitfire continued making inspection with his eyes and ears. His long, loose-limbed walk ate up the mile-long track. Trish pointed to the infield at a small yellow and white building with a red roof, topped by a curious weathervane of a jockey mounted on a horse.

"Bet that's the winner's circle." Trish stopped her horse so they could get a better look at the circle of low, perfectly trimmed shrubbery. Two rows of white picket fence led from the track to the circle. "We're gonna be in there a week from Saturday, ya hear?" Spitfire snorted and went back to walking.

The glassed-in grandstand reminded Trish of Portland Meadows, but it was in better shape. Morning sun reflected off the huge panes. Die-hard spectators trained their binoculars on the working horses.

Trish nudged Spitfire into a trot for the second circuit. His easy attitude seemed to say, "A track is a track. Nothing to get excited about."

Sarah's Pride didn't agree with him. When Trish took her out, she tracked every shadow and shied at a few of her own imagination. And she didn't want to walk. Her stiff-legged trot forced Trish to post and finally rise in the stirrups. The filly even shied away when another horse came up beside her.

Patrick had walked to the track with them so he could watch the work. He shook his head when Trish brought the sweating filly to a stop in front of him.

"I'm not sure who got more of a workout, her or me," Trish grumbled, but her smile and the way she stroked the filly's neck showed she didn't mean it. "You gotta settle down," she crooned to the filly's still-twitching ears. "You can't win any races if you use up all your energy before the gate opens."

Patrick stroked his chin with one hand. "I'm thinkin' we'll do blinders on her. And lots of galloping."

Trish nodded. "Hear that, girl? Patrick will turn you into a winner yet." She turned out the gate and followed the fence line back to the barn. Patrick remained behind to watch some of the other horses work.

Mel Howell met them after breakfast. "You ready for the grand tour?" His beeper squawked and he raised a hand while he spoke into the small black box. Then he smiled again. "Sorry for the interruption. Now, where were we?"

An hour and a half later Trish felt as if she'd been toured by a walking, talking, thoroughbred-racing encyclopedia. Mel showed them the grave of Barney, the track dog, in a corner near the Stakes barn. Then he led them up and down, around and through the grandstand complex, all the while sharing anecdotes from Pimlico history. When he walked them out to the infield area that Trish had admired earlier, Mel confirmed her guess. This was the winner's circle for the Preakness. The yellow and white building was the remaining cupola from the old grandstand that had burned years before.

"The blanket of flowers for the winner is woven of chrysanthemums, actually," Mel continued his flow of information. "We have to dye the centers to match the traditional black-eyed susans, because that flower doesn't bloom till later in the summer."

Trish shook her head. "At least no one has to worry about thorns like on the roses at Churchill." She remembered getting stuck by one the trimmers had overlooked. "Do you have bands and guards like they do there?"

"Of course. And extra guards around the Stakes barn as soon as the entries begin to arrive. Safety's my job, besides making sure all you celebrities feel comfortable here, and welcome."

Trish and David smiled at each other and then at him. "Celebrities?" Trish still didn't think of herself as one. At

Mel's nod, she shrugged and grinned again. "Whatever.
But thank you for all you've done for us. We've never had
a limo and driver before."

"You suppose this is what rock stars feel like?" David
asked after they returned to the barn and told Patrick
about their tour.

"I don't know." Trish stretched her arms over her
head. "But I kinda like it." She wrapped her arms around
Spitfire's neck as he leaned his head over her shoulder
in his favorite position. "How about you, fella?" Spitfire
bobbed his head, his usual plea for more scratching. "All
right. All right."

Trish had just bemoaned the fact of having to return
to the hotel to break open *War and Peace* again, when a
man introduced himself as an agent. "I talked with Jonathan Smith," he said, "and he told me to get you some
mounts if I could. One of my boys cracked a collarbone
yesterday and can't ride for the rest of the week. Would
you be interested in two races this afternoon?"

Trish felt a jolt of excitement. "Sure. I'm not licensed
in Maryland yet, though. Is there time?"

"If you hustle. Come on, I'll walk you through the
process. Or run you through, in this case."

"But I don't have enough money with me. Do I have
time to go back to the hotel?"

"Not really."

"Here." Patrick dug out his wallet. "You can pay me
back later." He handed her several twenties.

"Thanks, Patrick. Bet you didn't know you'd have to
be my guardian angel when you signed on for this job."
Trish blew him a kiss as she walked backward beside the
trotting agent. Together they jogged back toward the
grandstand where the offices were located.

At least this way I'll get to race this track before the Preakness, Trish thought as she slipped into the unfamiliar blue and black silks. She hadn't had a chance to meet either the trainer or the horse but it wouldn't be long now. She watched the first race of the day on the monitor.

At the call for the jockeys, Trish trotted up the stairs to the men's jockey room where the scale was located. A valet there handed her the saddle and weights to bring her up to the required 121 pounds. Off to one side she could hear a couple of guys talking—about her. Even her ears blushed as she felt the warmth spread all the way up from her toes.

"Good luck," the steward told her. At least he had a friendly smile on his face.

Trish sighed. *Oh well, this is probably what it will always be like at first. I'll have to prove myself at every track in the country, no matter how many races I win.* She trooped back down the stairs with the other jockeys for race two.

She felt at home in the saddling paddock, because like Portland Meadows it was located under the grand stand. She was in stall five.

Trish introduced herself to both the trainer and the owner. "I'm pleased to have you ride for me," the older woman of the two said, her accent definitely sounding south of the Mason-Dixon line. "We've been following your career with interest."

"Thank you," Trish replied. Strange wasn't the word for this situation. Usually, even if a woman partly owned a horse, a man was either in charge or was the trainer.

The younger woman grinned at her. "My name's Jennifer Hasseltine, and contrary to my appearance I've been training for the last eight years. Mrs. Bovier is one of my favorite owners. And Johnny Be Late," she stroked the gelding's gray neck, "is one terrific fella. The boards out there show him the favorite but we don't need the numbers to tell us how great he is."

The horse nuzzled Trish's hand for more after munching her proffered carrot. Trish looked the horse in the eye and saw both desire and a calm spirit. The gray held his head proudly, as if he knew what they were saying and agreed completely.

"He reminds me of old Dan'l at home. That gray horse taught me a lot about racing and horses in general." She scratched his cheek and up behind the ears. Johnny Be Late blew in her face.

"Riders up!"

After a knee up, Trish settled herself in the saddle and smoothed a stubborn lock of gray mane to the right side. She patted Johnny's neck in the process.

"He's a sprinter," Jennifer said, "and with six furlongs you better take him to the front and let him go. Watch out for number four; he should be your main contender."

Trish nodded. It *really* seemed strange to be taking orders from a woman, but she liked it.

The parade to the post gave her the same thrill here as at home. When the bugle blew she and Johnny were ready to perform. Her horse was all collected power as they cantered back past the grandstands and out to the starting gate. He walked into his assigned gate and waited like a true professional.

Trish slipped into her normal singsong that calmed both her and her mount. She felt him gather under her, and when the gate clanged open he was ready. He surged forward neck and neck with number four, and the two of them set the pace. Down the backstretch and into the turn, this was definitely a two-horse race.

Coming out of the turn on the outside, Trish relaxed her hold on the reins. The gray pulled ahead one stride, then another. Number four picked up the pace and drew even again.

"Okay, fella, let's get this over with," Trish sang to the flicking ears. This time Johnny pulled away, and kept pulling away. Each stride drove them farther ahead until they won by two lengths.

Trish gave the gelding his moment in front of the crowd. "See, fella, that's you they're cheering. You ran a fine race."

Jennifer grinned up at Trish as she led the horse into the winner's circle. "He's good, isn't he?" She scratched under Johnny's forelock. "You rode him well."

"He was easy," Trish said as she smiled for the photographer. She leaped to the ground and stripped off the saddle.

"You can ride for me anytime," Mrs. Bovier told Trish. "I like your style. You didn't need the whip and you didn't use it."

"Thank you, my pleasure." Trish felt a warm glow in her middle. It was nice to be complimented on something she believed in so strongly. She never went to the whip unless she was forced to.

The next race wasn't so easy. She found herself boxed in right from the beginning. Rather than drive between two horses that yielded only a slight opening, Trish pulled back and to the outside. She was still off the pace going into the final turn, but her horse lengthened his stride and drove down the stretch like a runaway locomotive. They passed two horses with one leading and with a furlong to go.

"Come on, you can do it!" Her words seemed to fly off on the wind. With all her encouragement, they pulled up to the stirrup, then the neck, and with one stride— Trish wasn't sure who won. Had his whiskers been over the wire first? Only the camera would tell.

"And that's number three, Hot Shot, owned by Springhill Farms and ridden by Tricia Evanston." The speaker sounded tinny but the message rang true. She'd won two at Pimlico. And this one surprised everyone.

"That was some ride," Patrick said when she joined him and David at the rail for the running of the seventh race.

"Cut it kinda close." David shook his head. "I think you've made your mark here at Pimlico."

The morning papers agreed.

"Kinda nice, wouldn't you say?" Trish asked Spitfire during their long gallop a bit later. Spitfire snorted. "All the publicity; you're famous now. How does it feel?" Spitfire shook his head. "Wish Red were here," Trish spoke her thoughts. "He's more fun to talk to than you." Spitfire snorted again. At the thought of their first kiss, Trish felt tingly in her middle. It would be nice to see Red again.

There wasn't much time for conversation on the gallop with Sarah's Pride.

"Tomorrow we'll run her with blinders." Patrick pushed back his hat and scratched his forehead. "She pulled out on you when that sorrel came up beside you. She always do that?"

"Seems to." Trish helped David finish scraping the sleek red hide. "Let's get done here, I'm starved."

That afternoon's program didn't go as well. Trish again had two mounts, but she only pulled off a place. In the other race she not only was boxed in, but the horse got bumped and finished second-to-last.

"Mom and Dad in yet?" Trish asked after a quick change in the jockey room. "I made reservations at a restaurant down at the inner harbor. The woman at the hotel desk said it was a really great place to eat."

"They're here," David answered. "But Dad's already gone to bed. Trish, he doesn't look good at all."

CHAPTER 7

"Not good" didn't begin to cover how bad Trish's father looked.

"Go ahead, wake him," her mother said. "He wants you to."

Trish crammed her fist against her teeth to keep from crying out. *How can he look so much worse? He hasn't even been gone a week.* She tiptoed forward to stand next to the bed. "Dad?" She touched the bruised hand lying on top of the covers. When Hal didn't respond, she turned a questioning look to her mother.

Marge nodded.

"Dad." Louder this time. Trish gently shook his shoulder.

Her father's eyelids fluttered. His eyes seemed sunken back in his head, and the skin of his face looked gray against the sharp cheekbones. He had lost weight again. It was obvious by the creases from his nose to the corners of his mouth. Slowly, as though moving against a heavy weight, Hal's eyes opened.

"Trish." He turned his hand to take hers. "Sorry I'm so tired." His voice faded in and out like an out-of-tune radio. "David, we—we'll talk in the morning, okay?" His eyes closed again before anyone could even answer.

Trish watched him breathe. Each breath seemed a

struggle, yet the effort hardly raised the blanket. *Where has my strong, dark-haired, laughing dad with the broad shoulders gone?* Trish thought. *The one who tossed me into my racing saddle as if I were a featherweight. The one who used to race me up from the barns at home? The man who knew God and trusted Him—my father.*

She stroked the back of his hand where an IV had infiltrated and left terrible bruises. His hands had always calmed both Trish and the horses. Now they looked too thin for any kind of strength. He coughed, but even in sleep he'd learned to be careful not to cough too hard.

Trish wiped her cheeks and eyes with her other hand. Marge handed her some tissues.

Trish had almost forgotten her mother and brother were there. All her love and strength focused on her father. She drew in a deep breath that snagged on the lump in her throat.

Then Trish heard the others leave the room. "God, you promised to hear our prayers, and we prayed for my dad to get better. You promised. You promised." Her whisper faded away as the tears chased each other down her cheeks.

Trish quietly left the room, then leaned against the door frame of the connecting living room. She crossed her arms and braced her fists under her armpits to keep from shaking.

"What's going on?" she pleaded with her mother.

"The doctors are trying a new method of treatment and your father reacted to it. He couldn't keep anything down for two days, but insisted we come ahead anyway. Then we couldn't get a direct flight, so the trip wore him out more than it should have."

"He looks terrible."

"I know. But a lot of that is because of exhaustion. He never sleeps well in the hospital."

"Why are they trying a new treatment?" David asked.

"I promised your father I'd let him tell you about this last week."

"Promises don't mean much," Trish blurted, then turned to her bedroom and closed the door behind her.

After changing into pajamas, she climbed into bed. Who cared about dinner? She didn't want to talk to anyone. With pillows propped behind her, Trish leaned against the headboard. *If Dad is getting better like we all thought, why the new treatment? If he isn't getting better, what's going on? Is he worse?* She thought back to the weekend before. He hadn't seemed worse. No coughing to speak of. He'd handled all the Derby stuff.

Trish tried to distract herself by examining her fingernails. None of this made any sense. Was God letting them down? She chewed on a torn cuticle until it bled. "Ouch." She pressed her thumb on the skin to stop the bleeding.

What scripture verses would help now? None came to mind.

Trish picked up *War and Peace*. Maybe reading would calm her mind. Half an hour later she dumped the book on the floor. She couldn't hear anyone in the next room. Her watch read 8:30. She snapped off the light and snuggled down under the covers. The Jacuzzi from Kentucky would be real welcome about now.

After rolling over and smashing her pillow for the umpteenth time, Trish turned the light on again. She glared at the ceiling where she was sure her prayers were floating. Where had God gone? Picking up the eagle, she smoothed the carved wings. Suddenly she threw back the covers, and carrying the eagle, tiptoed into her parents' room. She carefully set it on the nightstand where her father would see it when he woke up.

The door to their parents' room was still closed when she and David left for the track in the morning. Drizzly skies matched Trish's mood. A stiff wind blew the cold right through her as she galloped Spitfire and then Sarah's Pride. Even the horses seemed glad to get back out of the weather. It felt more like Portland than Baltimore. She couldn't have been prepared for weather on the East Coast. She'd never been there before. *And we probably shouldn't be here now,* she thought.

Trish finished her chores without speaking to anyone. Patrick gave up after one look at her face. David never tried. He didn't seem any better off than she was.

But by the time Hank Benson drove the limo through the gate, the sun and the clouds were playing a fast game of peek-a-boo. On the ride back to the hotel, Trish thought about Sundays at home. Chores, a good breakfast, and church. Then time to play with Miss Tee in the afternoon when the racing season was finished in Portland. She and Rhonda would probably go riding. The four musketeers would hang out somewhere. *Whatever we did, we would have fun. Even if it was studying together.*

Her last thought reminded Trish of finals. She'd better get in and hit the books again. She was only about three-fourths through the list, and all her assignments had to go back with David so he could bring her more. She shook her head.

"You okay?" David asked when they reached the door to their hotel suite.

"Yeah, sure." Frown lines deepened on her forehead. How could she be okay when her father looked so awful?

When they entered the suite it was like going through a time warp. Hal had showered and shaved, and was sitting up in a chair reading the newspaper.

"Good morning. Breakfast should be here any minute." His smile hid the lines Trish had seen the night before.

"D-Dad," Trish stammered in shock.

Hal teasingly touched his cheek, chin, and nose. "I think it's me. Last time I checked the mirror anyway." He laid the paper aside. "Haven't you a hug for me, Trish? I came a long way to get one."

Trish flew across the room and threw herself into his arms, with David right behind her. "But last night you—you looked—" She laid her head on his chest and soaked his robe lapel with her tears.

"I know, Tee. I know." He patted her back with one hand and reached for David's with the other. "I had hoped to get some rest so we could talk last night, but that trip wiped me out. Your mother and I really needed the sleep last night."

"The time change didn't help either." Marge stood beside them, her hand on David's shoulder.

There was a knock at the door. "That's breakfast. We went ahead and ordered for you. I knew you'd be starved." Marge went to open the door.

A waiter wheeled a white-clad table in, placed it in front of Hal's chair and raised two leaves, turning it into a larger, round table. He skillfully arranged the place settings, poured ice water in the glasses, and pointed out the items. There was a basket of rolls and muffins, two carafes of coffee, fresh-squeezed orange juice, milk, and plates of pancakes, bacon, eggs, and hash browns.

"Looks great," David said enthusiastically as he

moved chairs into place. He walked the waiter to the door and tipped him.

Trish lifted the silver lid from her plate. "It even smells good."

"Let's say grace together." Hal reached for Trish and Marge's hands on either side of him. Then David joined the circle.

"Father, we thank you for this food. Thanks too for a safe trip and for taking good care of our family. Thank you for a new morning, a new day in which to praise you. Amen." He opened his eyes and looked intently at each of them. "You have no idea how precious you are to me."

Trish bit her bottom lip to keep the tears from flowing. She lifted the silver dome again to inhale the aroma of fresh bacon and hotcakes. That bought her time to get the tears swallowed. She didn't want to cry again this morning. It was a time to be happy. They were all together.

She stole a peek at David. He was drinking his orange juice, not looking at anyone. Marge's hand covered Hal's, and her eyes were wet with tears.

"We sure missed you two," Trish managed. "But we made it. Things have been running pretty smoothly." She spread butter on her pancakes and poured syrup as though it were a typical Sunday morning. "I think Spitfire missed you, too."

Marge shook her head and quipped, "Too bad he couldn't have joined us for breakfast."

"Now that would not have been a bad idea," Hal said, waving his fork. "Then I wouldn't have to drive clear over there to watch him. And Trish would have more study time."

Trish shook her head and groaned. "Don't mention studying. Have any of you ever read *War and Peace*?"

"Yeah, it's a real snoozer." David poured coffee for himself, then his parents.

"It's a classic," Marge said, sipping her coffee. "A wonderful story."

Trish and David exchanged glances. Their eyes said *Parents!*

"Mother," David said seriously, "you'd have to be looney-tunes to love *War and Peace*."

"Thank you for that comment on my taste in literature. Coming from someone who thinks the funnies and the sports page are all that matters in a newspaper, I'm complimented."

Trish let her family's laughter and good-natured banter flow around her like a warm tide. She ignored the dark lines and gray tinge of her father's face. And when his trembling hands raised the coffee cup to his lips, she looked the other way. Nothing would spoil this moment for her.

The coffee drinkers were on their second cups, and Trish swirled the last bit of orange juice around the bottom of her glass. Wishing they'd ordered more, she relished the last drops.

"So, Dad, what's going on with you?" David asked casually.

David, how could you? Trish felt like screaming at him.

Hal pulled on an ear, and ran a finger around the rim of his cup. Finally he raised his gaze.

If Trish had never seen haunted eyes, she was seeing them now. She clenched her teeth against the pain she knew was coming.

"Well, the tumors in my lungs haven't grown any."

Trish let out the breath she'd been holding.

"But, they found—" Hal swallowed, then continued, "The cancer has metastasized; that is, it's traveled to somewhere else—to the liver and pancreas, in my case. That's why the doctors decided to try a new protocol."

Trish felt as if she were trying to swim to a surface that was out of reach. She was drowning.

"But—but I thought God was healing you! You said He always answers our prayers!"

"He does, Trish, He does." Her father leaned toward her. "Or I wouldn't be here now. Remember, they didn't hold out much hope last fall when they found the first tumors. And those shrunk."

"But now it's worse?" Trish stared into her father's dark brown eyes. "Is that what you mean?"

"I mean that we continue to pray. We know that God knows what He's doing—"

"Maybe you do, but not me. I don't know any such thing right now." Trish pushed herself to her feet, catching the chair before it toppled to the floor. When would she be able to breathe again? "Excuse me." Her voice stuck in her throat. She felt as if she were slogging through mud on her way to her bedroom. She closed the door carefully behind her, as if being quiet would change what her father had just said.

She collapsed on the bed, clutching a pillow under her chin. "God, you'd better not let my father die. You promised to make him better. I read those words, I even memorized them. You said, 'By His stripes you are healed.'" She beat her fist into the pillow.

"My Dad trusts you. You can't let him down." She rolled over and wrapped her arms around the pillow.

"You can't. You can't." She let the tears flow.

The pain in her chest clawed deeper. Was this what a broken heart felt like? She wiped her eyes and sat up. It seemed like hours had passed when she pulled off her boots and shoved her feet into her running shoes.

"I'll come with you," David said when she opened the door to leave.

"No!"

"Sorry, no choice. You can't run around here by yourself."

"You're not my boss!" Trish threw the words over her shoulder as she thundered down the stairs.

David never responded. He just kept a few paces behind her.

Trish's feet pounded the gravel, then the concrete sidewalk. She crossed a grassy field, ran up a hill; gasping for breath but refusing to stop. Downhill she picked up speed. At the bottom she slipped in a patch of mud but caught herself and ran on.

David dogged her steps. Trish could hear him struggle for breath, too. The challenge? To run David into the ground. Her sides screamed with pain—her lungs, her legs. Finally she dropped to her hands and knees under a tree—and threw up. She gagged and retched and heaved again till there was nothing left but a feeling of complete exhaustion.

When she could move, Trish crawled to the trunk of the tree and leaned against it.

David lay on the grass nearby, his face on his arms.

"You didn't have to come." Trish finally spoke.

"I know."

Trish sat with her back against the tree, her knees drawn up to her chest. She closed her eyes, listening—

for what? Her nagger could finally make himself heard above the poundings in her body.

You blew it again. Every time you hit a problem you blow it. Trish shoved herself to her feet. "Let's see about getting back. Any idea which way to go?"

David pointed to the left.

It *was* a long walk back.

For the next two days, Trish felt as if she were on a roller coaster. One minute she'd be up—mostly when she was at the track. Then all the fears would catch up and she'd crash down again. She gave up praying. Why pray when God wasn't listening anyway? Her Bible verses? Hardly! She gritted her teeth and kept on.

Working the horses, schooling Spitfire and Sarah's Pride, and studying. She smiled when she was supposed to, answered when people spoke to her, was polite when journalists asked her questions.

She even joked with the trainer for Nomatterwhat. He had a good sense of humor even if his horse didn't.

Trish could keep the mask in place. She knew she could. She *didn't* open her Bible. She *didn't* allow the songs in, and she stayed away from the carved eagle—and her father. The latter wasn't so difficult. He slept most of the time.

One night she found a familiar 3×5 card on her nightstand. Her father's usually bold printing was a bit shaky but the verse was plain. "I will never leave thee nor forsake thee" (Hebrews 13:5).

Ha! What a joke! Trish wanted to rip the card up. Instead, she stuck it in her history book. She could deal with this setback. After all, she was tough. Wasn't she?

CHAPTER 8

"Let him out for half a mile, no more," Hal told Trish on Wednesday morning. "The stopwatches will be on you."

Trish nodded. She smoothed Spitfire's mane to the right and stroked his neck. "Okay, fella, let's do it." She trotted him around the track and broke into a slow gallop just before the half-mile pole. As they passed the marker, she let him loose.

Spitfire showed top form as he fairly sizzled around the track. He was still picking up speed as they flashed past the finish line. Trish stood high in her stirrups to bring him back down. "Easy now. Come on, you know the rules. Save it for Saturday."

Spitfire shook his head. He wanted, needed to run—all out.

"Don't tell me, let me guess." Trish grinned at the three men who waited for her at the exit gate. Patrick and David both clasped stopwatches in their hands. "Wasn't he fantastic?"

Patrick nodded. "That he was, lass." He grabbed his hat just in time. Spitfire was getting sneakier in his hat tosses. "You black clown, you." Patrick rubbed the top of his bald head and settled the fedora back in place—firmly.

Trish couldn't help giggling. Spitfire wore his "Who-me?" look, his head slightly off to the side in case some-one planned on smacking him. David loved it when *he* wasn't the object of Spitfire's pranks. Hal leaned against the fence, a grin erasing the look of weariness that now seemed permanently grooved on his face.

"So, what do you think?" David asked after stealing a peek at his watch.

Trish concentrated. "Ummm—49 and three."

"Wrong. Forty nine and one," David gloated. "You're off by two tenths of a second."

"Your watch keeps getting more and more accurate, Tee." Hal stroked Spitfire's nose. "An accurate internal stopwatch is the one thing that sets *great* jockeys apart from the rest. Did you push him?"

"Not really. But I can always tell the time easier on Spitfire. I s'pose it's 'cause I know him so well." She leaned forward to give Spitfire a hug. He tossed his head and flipped David's Runnin' On Farm hat off in the proc-ess. Trish giggled again. "See you guys at the barn before we get into any more trouble here."

Trish caught herself humming on the walk back to the barn. No matter how hard she tried, the melody broke through: "I will raise you up. . . ." She rotated her shoulders to release some of the tension. If only she could be riding and racing all the time, without a moment to think about what was happening in the rest of her life.

While the Evanstons were skipping most of the fes-tivities of Preakness week, Thursday morning proved the exception. Trish and David finished up the chores quickly so they could join their parents and Patrick at the Sports Palace for the Post Position breakfast.

"Mr. Finley!" Trish was surprised to see him.

"It's Adam, remember? It's good to see you, Trish. You didn't think we would miss this, did you?" Adam and his wife, Martha, circled the white-clothed table to give Trish a hug.

"Hang in there," Martha whispered in Trish's ear.

Trish felt the familiar burning behind her eyes. She blinked it back.

"Mr. and Mrs. Shipson." Trish shook hands with the owners of BlueMist Farms.

"Congratulations on your riding," the silver-haired Donald Shipson told her. "Spitfire looks magnificent."

"Thank you."

"My dear, you are a credit to women everywhere," Bernice Shipson added in her soft Kentucky drawl. "We have a filly entered in tomorrow's third we'd like you to ride."

"Be glad to," Trish answered, smiling. This woman was easy to like. If Spitfire had to go to another farm, at least these people seemed like family.

Trish caught Patrick's nod of approval as she slid into the chair next to her father. He reached over and patted her hand, sending a warm glow all the way to her heart.

Crystal chandeliers, plush carpet, beautiful table settings, all set off the richness of the Sports Palace. Here the wealthy came to play, but Trish didn't feel out of place. Her family had earned their position here by right of excellence. Her gaze wandered to the gallery of oil portraits of jockeys who had won the Preakness. The display extended around the corners of the room. Would *her* picture join the elite one day?

Trish could feel her butterflies trying out their wings as the drawing got under way. They were seventh on the list of nine.

Nomatterwhat headed the list. The Steward drew number three. The numbers ninth, fifth, seventh, and eighth followed. Trish clenched her fists in her lap. Did they have to take so long between draws? A cheer went up. Equinox drew the post. The next number would be theirs.

Hal draped his hand across the back of her chair and gripped Trish's shoulder. She flashed him a quick smile and turned back to watch the draw.

"Position number two. Spitfire, owned by Hal Evanston." *Between Equinox and Nomatterwhat*, Trish thought. *One's a pain in the neck and the other our chief contender from the Derby.*

Trish dragged in a deep breath. At least they didn't have as far to run this time. They could take the pole and just run the others into the ground.

"That'll be good," Hal said. He nodded, and patted Trish's shoulder.

As soon as the final two numbers were called, the crowd was on its feet, including the media. Several reporters gathered around the Evanstons, questions tumbling out. Trish listened with one ear while David slipped away. She couldn't get away if she wanted to; her father stood, with his hand on her shoulder.

"What about your health, Mr. Evanston?" one of the reporters asked. "Could that keep you from running in the Belmont?"

Hal smiled. "We have to win here first. I learned a long time ago to take one race at a time. In fact, to take one day at a time. You can't live tomorrow until it comes. As to my health, I am in God's hands. There is no safer place to be. I trust Him absolutely to do what is best for me and my family."

"And the colt—Tricia, you ride Spitfire every day. His leg any problem?"

Trish lifted her chin and banished the tears that threatened at her father's words. She squared her shoulders. "Spitfire's in great shape. You know his time from yesterday, and there's been no swelling for weeks now. We're as ready as we can be."

"You'll be retiring him to stud at BlueMist Farms then, right after the Belmont?"

"That's the plan, but we haven't put a timetable on it yet," Hal answered.

Trish felt her father leaning more of his weight on the hand that rested on her shoulder. She glanced at her mother. Marge nodded, acknowledging that she knew what was happening.

Trish took a deep breath. "That's enough for today, folks. You know that we'll be around if you have more questions later. Thank you very much." She slipped her arm around her father's waist.

As the reporters left to search for other stories, Trish pulled out a chair with one hand and eased her father into it with the other.

"You did just fine, lass," Patrick spoke in her ear so only she heard him. "Good timing."

Trish stood with her hand on her father's shoulder while he talked with the Finleys and Shipsons. Marge had taken the chair beside him. Trish could feel her father's weariness under her hand. She wanted to throw both arms around him, to give him her strength, to fight off the disease that was causing him pain.

You've got guts, Dad, she wanted to tell him. *When you believe in something you both walk it and talk it. Standing up there like that announcing your faith to the world—and this isn't the first time.* She thought back to the ceremonies after the Derby. He'd given God the glory then, too.

On the way back to the barns Trish heard an argument going on in her head again. One side demanded she stay mad at God. The other insisted she needed all the strength only her heavenly Father could give her. And the courage her father had.

Courage. Guts. Peace. Her father had it all.

Trish had a lot of anger. And resentment.

She slipped into Spitfire's stall and slid down to sit in the straw in the corner. Spitfire nuzzled her hair, then cocked his back leg and dozed off again.

Trish crossed her arms over her bent knees and rested her forehead on her arms. She tried to pray, but the ceiling here seemed as tight as the hotel's. Why wasn't God hearing her?

You're still angry, her little voice slipped in now that things were quiet. *Tell Him about that.*

"So, God, I'm angry. I'm so mad I don't even want to talk with you. I just want to scream and pound things. I want to run away from all these problems and have them all better when I come back." Tears slipped down her cheeks and clogged her throat. "You can heal my Dad. I know you can. So why is he worse? I don't understand."

Spitfire wuffled in Trish's ear. When she raised her face, he licked the tears off her cheek. "Spitfire, I just don't understand." She rubbed the soft spot between his nostrils. "I don't know what to do. How can I have the courage my father has?"

She pulled a piece of hay out of the sling and chewed on it. "Do you think God's gonna help me?" She pulled the horse's head down lower so she could rub under his forelock. Spitfire closed his eyes in bliss. "Sometimes I don't much like God, you know."

She chewed some more. "Do you think Dad—no . . ."
She shook her head. "I haven't been very nice to him
lately—to anyone." She tilted her head back and stared
at the ceiling. Spitfire blew softly on her face and licked
away another tear.

"One day at a time. That's all I gotta take." Trish drew
circles on her knees with a fingernail. "Huh, one minute
at a time is more like it."

She sat silently for a while. Spitfire dozed off again.
"Jesus, please help me. I need you so badly." Her nose
ran and then her eyes. She wiped them on her sleeve.
But this time, bit by bit, the peace she needed so des-
perately slipped into the stall and snuggled around her
shoulders—and into the corners of her mind.

Patrick found Trish sometime later—curled up in the
straw, sound asleep.

The peace stayed with her all day and through the
night. When her nagger tried to get on her case in the
morning, she just shook her head and shut him down.

"Better today?" Patrick asked as he boosted Trish
into the saddle for morning works.

She smiled down at him. "Better."

That afternoon she met the Shipsons and their
trainer in the saddling paddock. Their filly sniffed Trish's
outstretched hand and up her arm to her head and shoulders. When she finished her inspection, Trish gave her a
chunk of carrot and rubbed the satiny bay cheek.

"You're a pretty nice girl, aren't you?" Trish murmured in the filly's ear. "You think we can take this race?
I do."

"She's in top condition," the trainer said. "Watch her,
because she likes to set the pace and can run herself out.
She placed at the Oaks; should have won it."

"Riders up!"

Mr. Shipson grasped Trish's knee and tossed her into the saddle. "She likes distance. I think the two of you will be a good match."

The blood-bay filly danced behind the lead pony. Head high, ears catching every sound, she listened to Trish's crooning and acknowledged the applause from the stands.

"You're a natural ham, aren't you?" Trish chuckled as the filly gave an extra bounce. On the canter back to the starting gates, the filly kept the pace with her lead pony, hoarding her strength for the race ahead.

"Good girl." Trish stroked the black mane and sleek red neck as they stood quietly in the gate waiting for the others to calm down. Trish gathered her reins and settled into the saddle.

The filly broke clean and fast. She had the post in three strides because the number one horse missed a beat at the gate. They had the lead going into the turn and there never was a serious contender. They won by three lengths.

"I don't know what happened to the rest of them," Trish said as she met the Shipsons in front of the winner's circle. "We just went for a fast ride all by ourselves."

"I said I thought the two of you would click," Shipson said as he led the filly into the winner's circle next to the grandstand.

After pictures, Trish looked across the heads of the crowd to the yellow and white building in the infield with the horse-and-jockey weathervane. *That's for tomorrow,* she thought as she leaped to the ground. *Spitfire and me. We'll take the Preakness—for my dad.*

CHAPTER 9

How can a morning like this feel so normal? Trish thought as she trotted Spitfire around the track. The rising sun had already burned off most of the fog. A wisp or two clung to the weathervane above the infield cupola at the winner's circle.

"Today's a big one," she announced as they passed the grandstand. "Middle jewel in the Triple Crown. You ready?" Spitfire snorted and jigged sideways. He tossed his head and pulled at the bit. "No, no running now. You save it all for the last sixteenth of a mile. That's when it counts."

Trish looked up at the grandstand with spotters already clinging to the fence. The yellow and black band underneath the glassed-in stands glowed in the morning sun. Each box logged two years, and the name of the Preakness winner for that year. Trish closed her eyes for a moment to picture *Spitfire* in big letters. Black on yellow.

"We can do it, fella. We can." They turned off the track and walked the easy rise to the Stakes barn.

"How's the lad?" Patrick asked when Trish dismounted.

"Ready."

"And the lass?" His grin crinkled his eyes.

"No butterflies." Trish laid a hand on her middle. "Hey, you guys sleepin' in there or what?" She stuck her tongue in her cheek and cocked her head. "Guess they are. How nice."

"Good. You just keep calm. The filly here is ready for a long gallop. Work some of the sass out of her."

By the time they returned, Trish could feel the work. Sarah's Pride had tried to pull Trish's arms right out of their sockets—all the way When Trish forced the filly down to a trot, the pace had pounded like a pile driver. The kid just wouldn't settle down and go easy.

"She can be a real handful," Trish said, rubbing her arms. "If we can get her to quit wasting her energy on nothing, we should have a winner." She stood in front of the steaming chestnut and looked the horse right in the eyes. "Shoulda called you Ain't Behavin' or some such. Whoever trained you—" She shook her head. "Well, they didn't do us any favors."

Sarah's Pride rubbed her forehead on Trish's chest. Tired, she needed some loving, not a scolding. Trish obliged as David and Patrick washed the horse down and scraped her dry.

As Trish thought ahead to the big event, her butterflies awoke and took an experimental flutter, as though warming up for the big one.

Hal joined them for breakfast. "How you doing this morning?" he asked Trish as they set their trays down at the formica table.

"Pretty good, actually," Trish answered. "Maybe I'm getting used to this or something." She spread strawberry jam on her toast. "What about you?"

"Other than three reporters already this morning, everything's fine." They shared a smile, then Trish heard a voice behind her:

"Excuse me. Tricia Evanston? May I ask you a question or two?"

Trish groaned but smiled as she turned around to face the reporter. "Sure. Be glad to."

"How do I feel this morning? Excited. Spitfire and me—we're ready. If all goes as it should, we'll have a real good race today."

"Boy, if you aren't getting the words down smooth." David poked her shoulder as he sat down beside her after the reporter had left.

"As they say, Davey boy, practice makes perfect." Trish sipped her apple juice.

"Naw, there's a new way to say that. Perfect practice makes perfect. And my sister is not perfect."

"Well," Hal added, "you have to admit she's been getting lots of practice."

"Yeah, but at what?"

Trish basked in the comfortable teasing pattern. If she didn't look at the lines on her father's face, she could pretend everything was all right.

But it isn't, her little nagger got his digs in. *So don't try to pretend. You're a big girl now; accept life as it is.* The butterflies seemed to agree as they took flying leaps, clear up into her throat.

Trish sighed. But instead of letting her shoulders droop, she straightened up.

"You okay?" Hal whispered.

Trish nodded. She swallowed the flutter in her throat. "Just my friends here." She patted her middle. "Guess they didn't want to miss the action after all."

She checked into the jockey room, armed with her schoolbooks. A wistful thought took her back to Churchill Downs and the women's jockey room there.

Here there weren't even windows. She felt as if she were in a box. The only contacts with the outside were the monitor and an intercom so she could hear the calls.

Trish settled into a chair and pulled out her assignment list. Only three things left to check off. Her history paper only needed a final draft, so she started on that. Copying didn't take a whole lot of concentration.

As the day's program flashed on the screen, Trish could hear the roar of the spectators. They'd already announced a record crowd for this running of the Preakness.

At race six, Trish put away her books and began to get ready. She polished her boots and sprayed her goggles, layering them on her helmet. Stretching took another fifteen minutes as she went through her routine, feeling the pull in each muscle with the hamstring stretches and curls. Lying back on the floor, breathing deeply, she closed her eyes. "Jesus," she prayed, "we both know this is a biggie. Help us do our best. But most important, make my dad stronger. Fight off the cancer for him. And like him, help me to give you the glory. Amen."

An arm over her eyes, Trish lay there. The same peace she'd found in Spitfire's stall was like a pillow under her now. God had heard her. She knew that for certain. And He cared.

At the call, she checked her appearance in the mirror. Spotless white pants, black boots, crimson and gold silks, and around her neck—an etched cross on a fine gold chain. She fingered the cross. It would have been nice to have Red here. One more friend to miss. Like Rhonda and Brad. She laughed at her reflection in the mirror. And then again, maybe not *exactly* like Rhonda and Brad. She saluted the mirror image and left the room, carefully closing the door behind her.

Once weighed in, she joined the other jockeys waiting for the call to go down to the horses. "Good luck," one of the men said.

"You, too." At the call, Trish followed them down the stairs and out across the dirt track to the turf course. Only during the running of the Preakness were the horses saddled in the infield. Yellow poles designated the spot for each entry. Spitfire waited by post two.

He nickered when he saw Trish.

"Missed me, did you?" she smoothed his forelock and rubbed his ears.

"We're praying for you," Hal whispered in Trish's ear as he hugged her.

David swallowed before he could speak. "Go for the glory."

Patrick waited beside the colt's shoulder. Trish started to shake his hand, but instead threw her arms around his neck and hugged him hard. "You'll do it, lass." She raised her leg to meet his waiting hands, and with a smooth, swift motion, settled into the saddle. When she looked down, she could see his eyes were suspiciously bright.

Trish sniffed and wiped her eyes. The smile she gave the most important men in her life rivaled the warmth of the sun. "I love you." She picked up her reins. "Okay, fella. Let's do it."

David led Spitfire, and Hal walked alongside with his hand on Trish's knee. As they stepped onto the dirt track, the pony rider met them. Hal gave his daughter one last pat as the bugler raised the shiny brass horn. The notes floated on the air. Parade to Post. The Preakness had begun.

Spitfire took the word "parade" to heart. Perfectly collected, neck arched, he jogged in step with his leader. The sun glinted blue on his shiny black hide. Muscles rippled, the mane and tail feathered in the breeze. Spitfire was everything a thoroughbred should be. He snorted at the turn and cantered back past the stands to thunderous applause.

"You know it, fella. They're yelling for you." Trish rode high in her stirrups, in perfect symmetry with her horse. When they approached the starting gate Spitfire waited his turn.

Equinox refused to enter the gate. It took four gate men to finally shove him into place.

Spitfire walked right in and stood perfectly at ease.

Nomatterwhat also needed encouragement. He'd acted cantankerous ever since the parade began, trying to outrun his pony and refusing to maintain his place in line. The remaining six filed into their assigned places.

Equinox reared in the stall.

Trish caught sight of the jockey bailing off rather than being squeezed between horse and gate. Spitfire stood still, listening to Trish's voice as she continued her soothing song.

One of the handlers led Equinox around and back into the gate. The jockey swung back aboard.

Trish breathed a sigh of relief and settled herself for the break. Spitfire tensed, his weight on his haunches, his focus on the track ahead.

The gates clanged open. "They're off!"

Spitfire broke in perfect stride. Equinox hung back. Nomatterwhat came into perfect sync with Spitfire. As they passed the grandstand for the first time, the two ran neck and neck, Spitfire on the inside.

Going into the first turn, Jones took Nomatterwhat into the lead by half a length. Trish kept a tight rein, letting the other horse set a faster pace. Through the backstretch they thundered stride on stride; Spitfire's nose seemed glued to Jones' stirrup. The remaining field spread out behind them.

Going into the turn, Trish loosed the reins a fraction. Spitfire's stride lengthened. He gained with each thrust of his haunches.

Jones went to the whip. Coming out of the turn, Spitfire paced him, stride for stride. But down the final stretch it was Spitfire going away.

Trish heard the thunder of Spitfire's hooves, his breath like a freight train. The crowd screamed, waves of sound bashing against their eardrums.

And it was Spitfire by one length. By two. The winner of the Preakness—Spitfire by three lengths. As they flashed across the finish line, Trish raised her whip in salute.

Tears streamed down her face. "Thank you, God. We did it. For my dad!" She listened for the announcer.

"And the winner of the Preakness is Spitfire—owned by Hal Evanston and ridden by his daughter, Tricia Evanston."

Trish and Spitfire cantered on around the track accepting the roar of the crowd as their due. At the sixteenth pole, an official opened the railing and waved her in. Trish trotted her horse back around the turf course, stopped Spitfire in front of the stands, and turned to face the crowd.

Head high, nostrils still flared red and breathing hard, Spitfire surveyed his kingdom. Trish stroked his neck, letting him accept the applause.

"It's ours, fella. Middle jewel of the Triple Crown. Your name is history now." She turned him toward the winner's circle where her family waited.

"Congratulations, Tricia." Mel Howell appeared beside her. He grasped the reins under Spitfire's chin and led them toward the cupola. White picket fences kept back the crowds and the press in the infield. Manicured shrubs outlined the flower-bordered circle. The huge silver Woodlawn Cup shone in its place of honor.

Trish smiled and waved till it felt as if her face would crack. She let the tears flow unchecked when she saw her parents, arm in arm in front of the red banner-decked porch of the cupola. Patrick and David met her at the circle.

David raised two fingers in what looked like a peace sign. Trish nodded. Two down.

"I know you could do it, lass. You and the clown here." Patrick thumped her knee and Spitfire's shoulder. He took the reins so Mel could help with the blanket of flowers. Yellow chrysanthemums with the brown painted centers, the blanket was draped over the horse's withers.

Trish felt the weight across her knees, like a heavy quilt. With one hand she smoothed the blossoms, waving with the other. Flashbulbs popped, video cameras recorded the moment.

Her father gripped Trish's hand. No words were necessary. The love and pride in his eyes said it all.

Trish leaped to the ground, right into her mother's arms. Marge hugged her hard, then wiped tears from both their cheeks.

Trish hugged Spitfire one more time before an official from the detention barn led him away to be tested. Mel motioned Trish to the scale, where once she was weighed, the race was declared official. She followed her family up to the railed podium.

Announcer John McKay, known everywhere as the voice of thoroughbred horse racing, first greeted them, then led them to the microphones. "And now, I give you the owner of this year's Preakness winner, Hal Evanston," his voice boomed over the applause of the crowd.

Hal stood a moment, surveying the sea of spectators. "I can't begin to thank you all enough for the way you've made us feel welcome here. Winning the Preakness with a colt from our own farm and my daughter riding it— well, it's beyond what most men dream of. I thank our heavenly Father for the privilege of being here, for keeping everyone safe in this race, and for my family, without whom none of this would be possible." He raised one hand to wave and clasped Marge to his side with the other.

"And now, the young woman you've all been waiting for—" McKay announced, pausing, "—winning jockey, Tricia Evanston! As you can see, they're keeping the trophies in the family."

Trish looked up at her father, then out at the crowd. She clenched the mike tightly in her hand to keep it from shaking. "Only one person a year gets to stand here for this honor. No one could be more proud than I am right now. Or more thankful. I have a lot to be thankful for. My father is standing here in spite of a killer disease. As he has said so many times, we are in God's hands." Trish choked on the last words. "There's no safer or better place to be. Thank you."

The crowd thundered again as she and her father hugged each other. They raised a replica of the Wood-lawn Trophy for another photo, but the one that would make most newspapers was the one of father and daughter in each other's arms.

"And now—" McKay introduced the Chrysler representative, who in turn presented a set of keys to Trish.

"These are for that red Chrysler LeBaron convertible waiting right over there. How does it feel to own two cars?"

Trish took the mike again. "It feels great and I love it. But this one's for my brother David." She grabbed his hand and stuffed the keys into it. "He earned it—the hard way."

"Trish, you can't—" David blurted.

"Oh, yes I can." Trish handed the mike back, and the crowd applauded again.

"I think she's got you, son," Hal said with a laugh. "You'll look good in it. Red seems to suit you both."

"Right. *Both* our kids in red convertibles," Marge moaned. "In Washington—where it rains all the time."

"Mo—ther." Trish and David echoed the lament of children everywhere.

CHAPTER 10

"And now the most important question—" McKay paused for effect. "Will you be going on to Belmont?"

"God willing," Hal replied. "We'll give Spitfire a bit of a rest and leave on Wednesday."

"And there you have it folks. Hal Evanston, owner of Spitfire, the winner of the first two legs of the Chrysler Triple Crown Challenge. Will this black colt be the first winner of the five-million-dollar bonus? We'll know in two weeks."

Hal, Trish, David and Marge waved again, then escorted by Mel Howell and several security people, trekked across the track and up to the Sports Palace for more celebration.

Trish watched her father closely. Was it exhaustion that made him look weaker or was it her imagination? Maybe they should just leave so he could get some rest. She stood behind him with her hand on his shoulder when he finally sat down.

Marge stood at his side. "Don't worry, Tee," Marge whispered under cover of someone else's question.

"Don't worry?" Trish whispered back, a smile tugging at the corners of her mouth. *Worrying is what got you into so much trouble. Must be a family trait.* Her thoughts flashed back to her grandmother at the Derby.

Now there was a worrier if ever there was one. When Trish looked back at her mother, she saw a younger form of her grandmother.

"At least I'm more like Dad's side of the family," Trish said in an undertone.

Marge raised her eyebrows.

"They don't worry so much."

Marge shook her head and chuckled. "No, I don't think you inherited the worry gene. I'm glad."

Then why do you worry? her little nagger leaped into the act. *You know better. It never does any good. Your worrying can't make your dad any better. In fact, it probably makes him worse.*

"Thanks a bunch," Trish muttered.

"What's that?" Hal turned his head to look up at her. He patted her hand at the same time.

"Nothing . . . I . . ."

"Well, Trish " Adam Finley took her hand. "We sure are proud of you. Martha and I . . . well, we feel you're part of our family now."

"And we couldn't be more pleased if you were our own daughter," Martha said as she gave Trish a hug.

"Thank you. Maybe being part-owners in Spitfire makes us all one family in a way."

"Family's better than business partners any day." Martha's blue eyes twinkled above a merry smile.

"You think you'll have any trouble deciding what to do with that five mil?" Adam teased Trish.

"We've gotta win it first, but it sure would buy a couple of good yearlings."

"Well, you certainly don't need to think about buying a car," Adam joked.

Trish laughed and glanced at her mother to catch her

reaction. They hadn't really talked about the convertibles yet. Her mother and father had always said "no car" until after high school graduation. And now she had two—that is, she and David. What if she won a third?

Hal patted her hand again. "What do you say we take a break here and head on back to the Stakes barn. David and Patrick could maybe use some help."

Things had quieted at the barns. Patrick greeted them, then finished talking with a reporter.

"How's it going?" Hal asked after sinking into a lawn chair. He tipped his head back and rotated his neck. When he opened his eyes again, Trish could tell it was an effort.

"The problem's back." Patrick sat down beside Hal. "Spitfire's foreleg is hot and swollen. We've got it iced, and tomorrow I'll start the ultrasound. He's had a nice feed. He earned it."

"How bad is it?"

"We'll know more in the morning."

"And the reporters?"

"They couldn't miss the ice pack."

Trish left them talking and slipped into the stall where David was refilling the ice pack that stretched from shoulder to hoof. "Want me to do that?"

"No, we're about done. How's Dad?"

"He looks so tired he scares me. But Mom says not to worry."

"Right." David rolled his eyes and shook his head.

———

The morning papers ran banner headlines: "Spitfire, Son of Seattle Slew!" The first line read, "Can he follow in his daddy's hoofprints?" Another article mentioned the recurring leg problem.

Trish read them all. The last winner of the Triple Crown was Affirmed in 1978, the year after Seattle Slew took it. There'd been only eleven winners in all the years of racing. Could Spitfire really do it? Could he win at a mile and a half, the length of the Belmont track? Trish's butterflies took a flying leap.

⎯⎯⎯

In the limo ride back to the track the next morning, a thought kept nagging at the back of Trish's mind. Maybe they should forget the Belmont and just ship home. In the long run it might be better for both her father and Spitfire. Both of them would get the rest they needed.

She resolved to bring it up when both Patrick and her father were together.

"How is he?" Trish asked as soon as she saw Patrick.

"Not good, lass." The usual twinkle was missing from his eyes. "But I'm not sure it's real bad either. From what your father says, the lad pulls out of this pretty fast. It's just that every incident may damage that muscle more." He stroked Spitfire's shoulder while he spoke. "I don't know what to recommend."

"Will shipping him make it worse?" Trish stroked Spitfire's nose that was already draped over her shoulder.

"Not to my thinkin'. As your dad says—"

"I know," Trish interrupted, "we'll take it one day at a time."

Patrick shrugged and nodded.

Dad looks so terrible. Trish's thoughts kept pace with

the filly's slow gallop. As if she sensed a problem, Sarah's Pride settled into the pace and maintained it without her usual fits and shies. As she rode, Trish's thoughts continued. She should be on top of the world, and instead she felt as if she were under it—holding it up.

"We sure enjoyed watching you win yesterday," Hank Benson told her on the ride back to the hotel. "My Genny was screaming, jumping up and down. I thought she'd burst her buttons when you entered the winner's circle. Says she wants to be just like you someday."

"You should have brought her out to the barn afterward."

"We knew you'd be busy. All those reporters and important people. I know what it's like for the winner." He smiled over his shoulder.

"Would you like to bring Genny along when you come to take us back to the track later this afternoon? She could meet Spitfire, maybe have her picture taken with him."

"You sure about that?"

"Sure. I'd love to meet her, too. I remember when I was twelve. I thought Bill Shoemaker was—well, movie stars have never been a big deal to me, but that man was."

"Yeah, he was the greatest. Shame about that accident. Just after he retired, too."

"I know." The limo stopped in front of the hotel entrance. "Tell Genny I'm looking forward to meeting her."

Hal was asleep again.

"He ate a good breakfast, though," Marge said. "He wanted to wait for you kids but he was too hungry."

"That's a good sign." Trish flopped in a chair. "How is he otherwise?"

"Yesterday wore him out."

"Yesterday wore us all out," David added. "I think I could sleep all afternoon."

After they'd finished breakfast, that's just what they did. Trish was amazed when she opened one eye to check the clock. *Four!* She stretched and yawned. So much for studying. The limo was due back in half an hour.

———

"Your dad says you take riding lessons," Trish said to Genny after they'd been introduced. "Tell me about them."

Genny sat in the seat with her back to the driver. She had long dark hair, held back by a red headband, and she wore jeans and a red turtleneck. She leaned forward as she spoke, her hands on her knees. After telling about her classes, she asked, "How do I get to be a jockey like you?"

"You keep riding, and when you're older start asking if you can exercise horses for one of the farms. You may have to clean stalls to get in, but keep asking. One time they'll need someone, and if you're good, you're on your way. There's one thing though—Do you like to get up early in the morning?"

Genny flinched a bit and wrinkled her nose. "Not really."

"Well, morning works start at 4:30 or 5:00, you know."

———

When they arrived at the track, Patrick was measuring the horses' evening feed. Trish handed Genny a couple of pieces of carrot from the bag in the cooler.

Spitfire nickered as soon as he heard Trish's voice. He reached his nose out as far as he could to greet her, a soundless nicker fluttering his nostrils.

"You old silly." Trish rubbed his nose and smoothed his forelock. With one hand gripping his halter, Trish motioned Genny closer. "Spitfire, meet Genny." Spitfire reached out and sniffed Genny's arm and up her shoulder. He inspected her hair, then down to her palm where he lipped his carrot and munched.

"I think he likes you," Trish said.

"He likes anyone who brings him carrots." David leaned on the handle of his pitchfork. With a quick motion, Spitfire sent David's crimson and gold baseball hat floating to the ground. "Spitfire, you—you!"

"You should have brought him a carrot," Genny said innocently, a gleam dancing in her eye.

"Thanks." David grinned at her as he bent over to pick up his hat. "Just be glad you're not wearing a hat."

"How about if your dad takes a picture of you and Spitfire?" Trish asked.

"And you?" Genny wondered.

Trish nodded. "If you like." Trish turned her back so Spitfire could drape his head over her shoulder. Genny stood on the other side of the horse. Hank took several shots, reminding them each time to smile.

Genny's grin dimmed the lights. "Thank you, Trish. And Spitfire." She fed him her last bit of carrot. "You're the neatest."

On the way back to the hotel, Genny asked Trish to sign her program from the day before. By the time they parted, Trish felt almost as if she had a little sister. "You write to me now," Trish said, "and keep up your lessons. Maybe we'll be riding in the same race someday. You never know."

Trish let out a sigh as she and David entered the hotel. Spitfire hadn't gotten any worse. Maybe they should go on after all.

"You did good." David tapped her on the shoulder.

His praise flew straight to her heart. "Thanks. I needed that."

Hal listened carefully that night when Trish suggested they might all be better off if they flew back to Portland rather than continue on to Belmont.

"What do you think, David?" Hal asked.

David paused, his forehead wrinkled in thought. "I'm not the one that's sick. We won't know about Spitfire's leg, but it could be fine in the next couple of days. It's you we're worried about."

That word again, Trish thought. *From now on the "w" word should be outlawed in our family.*

"Marge, what about you?"

"You're awfully close to your dream to quit now."

Trish stared at her mother. She could feel her mouth drop open—and stay that way.

"Patrick?" The trainer had joined them for dinner.

"I can't be walkin' in your shoes. Who but God can know the future?"

Hal leaned back in his chair, his fingers steepled under his chin. The light from the lamp slashed deep shadows in his face. Trish shuddered. He'd lost more weight, she was sure of it.

"One day at a time," he finally said. "We're in God's

hands—one day at a time. We'll make the final decision on Tuesday night."

It rained all day Monday. Trish spent the time studying. David and Patrick kept doctoring Spitfire's leg. Hal slept. Marge stayed busy knitting a sweater.

Before she went to sleep that night, Trish finished reading *War and Peace*. Now she just had to write the report and the assignment list was finished. Her prayers remained the same. "Please make my dad better. And Spitfire, too."

On Tuesday the rain continued. Hal polled them all that evening. After listening to everyone's comments, he announced, "We leave for Belmont at 9:00 A.M."

Trish wasn't sure if she was happy or sad.

———————

Both horses loaded without any trouble in the morning. Spitfire wasn't limping but the leg was still warm to the touch.

Trish felt that old familiar lump in her throat as she said goodbye to Mel Howell and their limo driver, Hank Benson. "You made me really feel good here," she said. "You sure you don't want to come along to Belmont?" After shaking hands, she climbed up in the cab of the horse van. The driver wasn't friendly like Hank or Fred Robertson.

Trish turned in the seat to get a last glimpse of Pimlico as they pulled out of the long drive. A new rental car followed right behind them with David driving.

Trish settled back in the seat. Her father had said they'd be there in about five hours. She rolled her jacket up and propped it against the window. Any time was a good time to catch a few extra Z's.

Trish wasn't sure how long they'd been driving, but she'd awakened as they crossed the river and entered the New Jersey Turnpike. Paying to drive on a freeway was a whole new concept to her. So far they'd stopped several times to pay the toll.

Up ahead construction warning signs flashed. A lighted sign overhead posted the speed limit and how far the slow-down would last. She settled back against her jacket.

Then the screech of brakes jerked her fully awake. Lights from the car ahead fishtailed in front of them. The van driver hit his brakes and in the same motion swerved to the left to avoid an accident.

Another car crashed into the rear of the truck. The screeching and rending of metal pierced the air. Trish felt her body slam against the seat belt, and her head hit the side window.

Was it David who crashed into us?

Then she heard Spitfire scream, and everything was silent.

CHAPTER 11

The blow to Trish's head left her dizzy. All she could think of was Spitfire. Was he hurt? Or just frightened?

Trish unsnapped her seat belt as soon as the truck came to a halt, and with a groan she pushed the door open and dropped to the ground. Her shoulder had apparently hit the side window, too.

"Easy, fella," she called. *How do I get the van door open?* Everything was tipped at a crazy angle. She could hear the horses shifting and sliding around. Then she thought of the driver and dashed around the front of the truck and pulled the driver's door open. He was slumped against the steering wheel, but at least he was breathing, and moving slightly. "You okay?" she whispered, not seeing any blood.

"I think so," he managed. "Check on the horses."

Spitfire! I've got to get to him. Trish ran to the back of the van. It was then that she saw the smoking car with the front end pushed in. At least it wasn't their rental car.

By this time Trish could hear car doors slamming. Someone was moaning—or crying. She could also hear the horses snorting, their hooves thudding as they scrambled to find footing on the slanted floor. Trish clambered up the side of the van, bracing her feet in the slot that held the ramp. She reached the door handles but gravity sucked the doors shut. No matter how she strained, she couldn't open them.

Then Spitfire screamed again.

Trish wiped moisture from her right eye. When she glanced down she saw blood on her hand. She tried to keep her voice firm but fear made it wobble. She sucked in a deep breath. *Where are David and Patrick? Are they hurt, too? God, please help us!* "Easy, fella, take it easy now," she spoke through the doors, but her voice broke on a sob. "Come on, Spitfire, just stand still until I can help you."

What were only minutes passing seemed like hours to Trish. She tugged again on the door handles. For once in her life, she wished she were taller.

"It's okay, Tee." David pulled himself up beside her. "We'll get it open." He grasped the handles firmly. "Now when I lift, you grab the edge. Together, we can do it." David worked from the ramp slot and Trish dropped to the ground. When he cracked the door, she threw her weight into the effort and pushed it upright. David shifted position and the door fell open.

Trish scrambled into the van. At the sight of her, Spitfire whinnied and Sarah's Pride slipped, thudding her knee against the wall of her stall.

"Easy now, you two," Trish crooned. Her voice choked when she saw blood flowing down Spitfire's cheek from a gash above his eye. Wild-eyed, he snorted and lunged against the tie ropes. The acrid smell of smoke drifted in from the smoldering car, and Trish sneezed as she fumbled for the ties.

"Here, let me help you." David jerked one lead free. "Let's turn them both so they face up the slant. Then they should be able to stand without slipping around."

Together they backed Spitfire out of the padded stall and faced him toward the door.

"Where's Patrick?" Trish asked as she stroked Spitfire's neck and face. The colt shuddered under her soothing hands.

"With Dad and Mom. The driver of the car that rear-ended you is hurt pretty badly. Hold on to Spitfire and I'll go tell Mom and Dad you're okay. Then I'll come back for the filly."

In what seemed like seconds, David was back in the van. "Okay, girl, let's get you moved out, too." He eased Sarah's Pride back and let her gain her footing.

By the time both horses were calmed down, Trish could hear sirens approaching.

"How's your driver?" David nodded toward the front of the van.

"Pretty groggy, but I didn't see any blood. He said he thought he was okay." Trish wiped her face again. This time she flinched.

"You better leave that alone," David said. "Looks like it's quit bleeding."

"How's Dad?"

"I'm not sure. We told him to stay in the car, but you know Dad. Once I pulled the driver from the crashed car, Mom took over, and I came to help you."

"Where's all the smoke coming from?"

"The car behind us. I thought it was going to blow up. We used a fire extinguisher he had in the trunk."

Trish shuddered. "David, how bad was this accident, anyway?"

"I'm not sure," David answered. "Three or four cars were involved, at least."

Spitfire leaned his head against Trish's chest smearing blood on her shirt. Trish rubbed his ears. *Where else is he hurt? How about his leg?* The questions raced through Trish's mind like a rabbit evading a hungry wolf.

A state patrolman appeared at the door. "You kids okay in there? How about the horses?"

"You'd better check on the van driver. Anything here can wait," Trish answered.

"This could have been really bad, Tee." David rubbed the filly's ears and neck.

"Our guardian angels were working overtime again?"

"For sure."

More sirens could be heard in the distance. Spitfire shifted uneasily, but Trish was able to calm him again.

"It's like we're in no-man's-land. Why doesn't someone come and tell us what's happening?" Trish blinked against the pain that thudded by her right eye. She was beginning to feel panicky. "How is Dad?"

Just then Patrick stuck his head in the door and swung himself up into the van. "The ambulance finally got here." He looked at Trish. "You'd better let the medics have a look at you, too." He patted both horses. "Looks like Spitfire got clipped good," he murmured, inspecting the gash. "Anything else?" He turned to Trish again.

"I don't know. We haven't checked under the sheets."

Patrick looked at Spitfire's legs first, then the filly's. "Okay so far." He rolled back the crimson sheet. The colt flinched when Patrick touched his right shoulder. He carefully probed the area. "Pretty bad bruise. Maybe a pulled muscle. Has he been favoring this leg?"

"Not really, at least I don't think so." Trish tried to think about when they moved the horses. "No, he was moving pretty freely."

Patrick checked over the rest of the colt's body, then started on the filly. "Her knees are a bit skinned. That's all I can find now. It's a miracle, that's what I say."

"How's my dad?" Trish finally asked.

"Last I saw, he was directing traffic. He's the one who found someone with a car phone and called for help. Between your mother and David—well, the man behind you will be thankin' them for his life."

"What was the matter with him? Why'd he follow so close? You'd think he'd know better. Signs had been flashing for—"

"Now, lass," Patrick soothed, "let's just be thankful it wasn't any worse."

"I knew we should have gone home. Spitfire probably won't even be able to run, and Dad sure didn't need all this."

"Knock it off, Tee," David ordered. "Let's just get through this, and then we'll have time to sort it all out."

"Time? We *never* have enough time for anything."

David ignored her.

Trish leaned against a stall post. Suddenly she was too tired to think or move.

An Emergency Medical Technician from an ambulance spoke to them at the van doors. "I hear we have a head wound in here." When he saw Trish, he smiled. "I guess you're it. How about letting those two guys handle the horses, and you come out here where we can check you over?"

Trish handed the lead to Patrick. She stroked Spitfire's nose. "Now, you behave, you hear?" she spoke firmly to him. She almost jumped down, until her pounding head made her think better of it. She sat carefully on the loading edge of the van and let the EMT help her to the ground.

"Anything hurt besides your head?" the young man asked as he flashed a light in each of her eyes to check for dilation of the pupils.

"My shoulder's sore, but that's all. And I've had a concussion before, so I know what one feels like. This isn't it." Trish felt limp and drained—like a balloon with the helium gone out.

"You can sit down." He unfolded a collapsible stool. "This is going to sting some, but we need to clean the wound. It isn't deep; head wounds tend to bleed a lot." He opened gauze packs and antiseptic as he spoke.

A woman in uniform came up and slapped a blood pressure cuff on Trish's arm. "Mmmm—you're gonna have a shiner there. Just missed your eye. What'd you hit, anyway?"

"The latch on the wind-wing window, I think."

"I take it you were wearing your seat belt."

Trish nodded.

"Blood pressure's fine. How'd you get so much blood on your shirt? You couldn't have lost that much."

Trish winced when she shook her head. "No, my horse got a gash above his eye, too. If he wasn't so black, he'd have a shiner tomorrow like mine."

"Aren't you Tricia Evanston?" A man with a camcorder on his shoulder flashed a press pass. "And your horse, Spitfire—is he injured?"

"We're both okay. You can check with Patrick inside the box." Trish winced again at the sting of the antiseptic.

"Close your eye," the EMT ordered.

Trish followed his instructions. It felt good to be taken care of.

"There, I've butterflied the wound together. You may

want to have stitches, but it isn't an area that takes a lot of stress. Some doctors don't like to put in facial stitches unless it's absolutely necessary." He finished taping a gauze pad in place, then took an ice pack out of his bag and smacked it to start the chemical reaction. "Here, you better ice it."

Trish put the ice pack to her face. She could feel it turning cold as the chemicals worked together. "You have one of these for Spitfire, too?"

The young man laughed and smacked another pack. "Sure. Any horse that's this close to the Triple Crown deserves an ice pack if he needs it." He handed it up to Patrick.

Trish looked up to see her parents coming toward the van. "Hi! Are you guys all right?" Smiling hurt the side of her face. "Ouch!"

The EMT handed Trish a glass of water and two white tablets. "Here, these will help the pain."

Trish swallowed the tablets and stood to receive her mother's embrace. "Some trip, huh?"

"Are you all right, Trish?" Marge asked.

"I'll be fine, Mom. It's just a scratch."

Hal came to Trish's other side. "Thank God it wasn't any worse. Looks like you could have a shiner, though, Tee."

"That's what they say."

"Take it easy for the next day or two," the EMT told Trish as he folded his kit away and started to leave. "And I hope you win the Belmont."

"Thank you!"

"And thank you for taking care of her," Marge added. "All of you have been wonderful."

"You take some credit too, ma'am. You and your son

did just the right thing. If that car had blown—" He left, shaking his head.

As the last ambulance drove away, tow trucks arrived, and Trish climbed back up into the van to hold Spitfire while the horse van was pulled back onto the highway. It wasn't long before another driver arrived to replace the one who'd been taken to the hospital.

Trish, David, and Patrick settled the horses again.

"We'll stop for lunch at the next rest stop," Hal said before climbing back into the car. "I think we all need a break. Trish, do you want to ride in the car and let Patrick take your place?"

"No, Dad. I don't want to leave Spitfire. We'll be fine." Trish climbed back into the truck cab. She looked down at the front of her shirt. "Looks like we've been through a war or something."

The new driver, named Sam, agreed with her. He was an older man with a ready smile.

They didn't take a long lunch break, but it was still rush hour on Long Island as they neared New York City. Trish tried to catch a glimpse of the Statue of Liberty as they crossed the Verrazano Bridge, but it was too hazy. Sam pointed out sights as they drove up the Shore Parkway. Trish saw the signs to Coney Island, then the tops of the amusement rides off to the right. They passed JFK airport where more construction slowed the already bumper-to-bumper crawl.

After they exited the Cross Island Expressway, it seemed to Trish as if they passed Belmont Park signs for miles of almost country-like road before they turned in at gate six. Sam stopped at the guard gate and flashed his pass.

The uniformed guard consulted his clipboard. "Go

on down Gallant Fox Road and turn left on Secretariat Avenue. Runnin' On Farm will be sharing barn twelve with BlueMist Farms. We expected you long before now."

"There was an accident on the New Jersey turnpike," Sam told the man. "It took me some time to get there to replace our other driver."

"Everything okay?" The guard peered into the truck.

Trish felt like sliding to the floor. She knew how bad she must look.

News traveled faster than the speed of the van, because a crowd gathered around the west end of barn twelve. Trish waited until David opened her door.

"I don't want any more pictures," she whispered as she slipped to the ground. "Stay with me, okay?"

David nodded, but Trish could tell by the look on his face that he thought she was just being a typical girl. Flashbulbs popped when she and Spitfire appeared at the head of the ramp. The colt was limping noticeably.

CHAPTER 12

"How bad do you think it is?" Trish asked as Patrick probed the colt's shoulder and examined the muscles down his right leg. "Wouldn't you know it, the same leg got it again."

"Better'n two lame legs, though." Patrick ducked under Spitfire's neck and checked the other side. "Let's get 'em settled in and the ice packs in place. I'll start the ultrasound in the morning."

Trish measured grain and carried the buckets to each of the stalls. Her right shoulder ached with the strain, and her head pounded. She felt like hiding somewhere and letting the tears roll. *Like that would do any good*, she thought.

David had taken their parents to the Floral Park Hotel where Hal had made reservations. That left Trish to walk the filly to loosen her up. Once around the sandy aisle of the long green barn was enough.

When she got back, one of the grooms from BlueMist Farms was helping Patrick with Spitfire's ice packs. Two others had moved the Runnin' On Farm equipment into an empty stall.

Trish breathed a sigh of relief. Her father had been right. They really did need more help. Sarah's Pride stuck her nose in the feed bucket and switched her tail.

She already seemed to feel at home.

Trish leaned against the wall in Spitfire's stall while he ate. She was too tired to volunteer for the moving process. Spitfire lifted his nose and blew the smell of sweet feed in Trish's face, along with several flakes of grain. "Thanks. You're a big help, pal." She wiped her face with one hand and flinched when she touched the bandage over her eye.

"That place is just too far from the track," David grumbled when he walked back into the barn. "It felt like we drove on forever."

"There aren't many decent hotels around here anymore," Patrick said. "This area has really gone downhill the last few years. Most of the hotels are out by the airport."

"Were you able to get a place on the grounds?" David asked Patrick.

He nodded, checking the ice pack again without looking up. "That I did. Now, why don't you two take dinner back to the hotel and get some extra shut-eye. The lad here won't be workin' in the morning, so you can take your time about showing up. We have to be off the track by 9:30."

Trish checked Spitfire's eye again. Now that it had been cleaned up, she could tell it was just a surface wound.

"I'll put some antiseptic on that when he's finished eating," Patrick said. "Be on your way now."

Holding her head up was too much effort, so Trish let it fall against the headrest on the back of the car seat. They stopped for tacos at a fast-food place. While the food smelled good, Trish hardly felt like eating anything.

At the hotel, they found Hal sound asleep. Trish ate

half a taco and shoved the rest away. "Mom, can you fix me an ice pack? I'm going to bed." She only woke enough to mumble "thanks" when Marge came into the room and removed the pack an hour later.

In the morning Trish gasped at the freak that stared back at her in the mirror. Her right temple and upper cheek had swelled and turned a reddish-purple. The puffiness nearly closed her eye.

Her shoulder felt better after a hot shower pounded the stiffness out. She rotated it. "Ouch!" *Guess I won't do that again. Maybe I'll let David ride the filly this morning.* She looked longingly back at her bed.

David thumped on the door. "Come on, there's work to do. And I'm hungry."

At the thought of food, Trish's stomach rumbled. "I'm coming." She grabbed a windbreaker and checked the mirror one more time. "Yuck!" She stuck her tongue out at the reflection and dashed out the door.

"How is he?" she asked Patrick as soon as she walked into the barn.

Patrick raised an eyebrow. "I'm a-thinkin' he's looking a sight better'n you, if you don't mind me sayin' so."

"Thank you, that's just what I needed this morning." Spitfire nickered his welcome. "How ya doing, fella?" Trish stroked his cheek. With the brown canvas pack on his leg and the swelling above his eye, Spitfire didn't look like a stakes-race contender. Especially not the mile-and-a-half Belmont. They only had ten days to go.

"Well, see you later," Trish said, tickling the whiskery spot on her horse's upper lip. "I gotta take care of the girl here."

Sarah's Pride seemed content to walk today. They followed other horses down the narrow, tree-lined street to the entrance to the track. Some farms had hanging flower baskets decorating the overhangs of the white-trimmed barns. The grass along the curbs was neat and lush.

It was all Trish could do to keep her mouth shut. The place was incredible. And she'd thought Churchill Downs was big. "What do you think that noise is?" she asked David as he plodded beside them.

"You got me. Sounds like high-powered sprinklers of some kind, but I don't see any."

"Could it be crickets?"

David shook his head. "They don't make *that* much noise."

Trish stopped the filly beside a traffic guard at the crossroads. "What's all that noise we hear?" she asked.

The guard looked surprised, then a grin split his face. "Ah, them's cicadas."

At the look of bafflement on Trish's face, he explained. "They's a large insect in the elm trees. You hear 'em in the spring and summer when the weather turns hot."

"How do you spell what you called them?"

He wrinkled his brow. "C—sounds like an s; then i, then c—sounds like a k; then a-d-a. Accent in the middle, on the c-a. Where you from?"

"Washington."

"D.C.?"

"No, state."

"Ah-h-h, then you must be Tricia Evanston. Hear you had an accident yesterday. That colt of yours gonna make it?"

"Time'll tell," David answered for Trish.

"Well, good luck to you." The guard tipped his hat. "And welcome to Belmont."

"Thanks!"

Trish left David and guided Sarah's Pride through the gates. The mile-and-a-half track seemed twice as big as any Trish had known. Portland Meadows, backside and all, would have fit nicely on the infield. The grass and shrubs were neatly trimmed, and a couple of ponds glinted in the sunlight out beyond the tote boards.

And the grandstand. "Wow! Can you believe all this?" Trish said to no one. The filly shook her head. The wide concrete pad in front of the cantilevered stands reminded Trish of Santa Anita. She could see three levels of seats with only the top one glassed in. Flower boxes with trailing plants graced the front of the second level all the way down to the open seats.

The lighted tote board read WELCOME TO BELMONT PARK.

Trish clucked the filly into a trot at the far turn. A breeze carried a woodsy smell from the trees that lined the track. As the filly trotted up the far side, Trish caught a glimpse of houses through the trees. Otherwise, it felt as if they were out in the country. Two other tracks lay off to the left as they rounded the final turn, then more barns came into view.

"Can you believe it?" Trish asked David when he met her at the exit gate. "This place is huge."

"You haven't seen half of it," David said, walking beside them. "It's like a town all its own. Only instead of houses, the streets are lined with barns."

———

Back at the hotel, Hal didn't feel up to doing the

necessary paperwork yet, so Trish hit her schoolbooks. Marge had brought her more homework assignments, including a Shakespearean play and two more history papers to write. Because Trish wouldn't be in class, her teacher thought written papers would make up for the lectures.

"How're you doing?" Marge tapped on Trish's door later in the afternoon.

Trish groaned. "Come on in, Mom. I can't begin to keep all these characters straight." She slapped her hand on the cover of *King Lear*. "Why couldn't we at least have had one of the comedies for a change?"

"I remember reading one of the historical plays," Marge said. "We had a slumber party and everyone read the different parts. Even Henry IV can be pretty hilarious at three in the morning." Marge sank down in the chair across from Trish at a small table.

"Then what did you do?"

"Well, it was the night before the final, so we all trooped off to class and wrote like mad. Then I came home and crashed."

"Did you pass?"

Marge raised one eyebrow. "I got an A. That's the best way to study Shakespeare." She ran her fingers through her hair. "If I can find a *King Lear* at the bookstore, I'll help you if you'd like."

"If we can find a bookstore."

"That too. You want a Diet Coke or something?"

Trish chewed on the end of her pencil. "Sure. How's Dad?"

"Sleeping." Marge rose to her feet. "I'll be right back. You want anything else?"

"Another ice pack?" Trish pushed gingerly at the

bandage over her puffy eye. "Maybe I should wear a mask or something."

Marge shook her head and left quietly. She returned a short time later with soda and ice pack in hand. "Why don't you lie down with this for a while, Trish." She applied a damp washcloth first, and then the ice pack. "Thank God it missed your eye."

"I know." Trish closed her eyes and let the cold seep in. It felt so good.

The next day, after morning works, Hal appeared at the barn. "Let's go get the paperwork done, David. We can drive over there. We'll pay the fees and then scratch later if we have to. Patrick, how does he look?"

"I've been using the ultrasound and ice. Think we'll walk him a little this afternoon to limber him up some; see how badly he limps."

"I know you're doing everything you can. What do you think about that maiden race for fillies and mares on Wednesday for Sarah's Pride? Do you think she's ready for that caliber of field?"

Patrick thought a moment. "Either that or another claimer. She needs a race pretty soon. Uh-huh, that'd be a good one for her."

"Well, let's get over there," Hal said. "You ready to come now, too?" he spoke to Patrick.

As Trish started to climb into the car, Shipson's trainer, Wayne Connery, stopped her. "We have a filly running this afternoon. Would you like the mount? Are you licensed yet?"

"On my way right now, and I'd love to ride her. What race?"

"Fourth. That okay?"

"Great. See you then." Trish plunked herself back against the seat. "All right!"

Hal turned to look over his shoulder. "Are you going to be able to wear goggles over that cheek?"

Trish fingered the bandage. "I think so. It won't be the worst thing I've raced with. Glad I've been around the track a couple of times."

Patrick consulted his racing form. "That race is six furlongs. You'll start halfway up the backstretch. One long, easy turn."

"Cinch."

And it was. Trish took the filly into the lead from the first and won going away. She accepted congratulations from the Shipsons and leaped to the ground. The winner's circle at Belmont sparkled like a movie set. Potted plants bloomed everywhere, and there were brick risers that made it easy to get a crowd in the picture. There was even an awning over the scale.

"I could get to like this," Trish told David that evening.

————

Saturday morning Hal suggested they all ride the train into New York City and take a bus tour of Manhattan.

"You sure you feel up to it?" Trish questioned.

"We'll take it easy. Who knows when we'll get back to this side of the country."

Trish looked at her mother, who had the same question in her eyes. Marge nodded.

By the end of the day Trish thought her jaw must be double-hinged, it dropped open so many times. Grand

Central Station arched high above them till the ceiling seemed to disappear in the dimness. People rushed every which way to trains, and there were shops along the corridors.

The Grayline bus tour lasted five short hours and took them down Fifth Avenue from Harlem to Battery Park, where they could see the Statue of Liberty in the harbor. They passed Central Park, museums, luxury hotels, and numberless skyscrapers of every description.

"I've never seen so many tall buildings," Trish said in awe.

"That's because nowhere else *has* this many high rises." The tour guide grinned at her. "Only Manhattan Island was formed from bedrock that's a base strong enough for all the buildings." From upper, to midtown, to lower Manhattan the sights continued. Fifth Avenue, Broadway, Rockefeller Center, the famous names rolled off the guide's tongue.

"That's where the glittering ball falls on New Year's Eve." The guide pointed to a building on Times Square. "You've seen it on TV, I'm sure."

Trish nodded as she craned her neck to see Madison Square Garden. "That's the entrance?" She couldn't believe her eyes. All the things she'd heard of happening there, and the front of it looked like a second-rate theater marquee.

At the end of the tour, Trish sighed. "There's just too much to see here. We need to come back again."

"We could go to the theater," Marge said wistfully.

"Or shopping!" Trish enthused. "Wouldn't Rhonda love to go shopping here?"

David shook his head. "Not me. Where are we going for dinner? I'm starved."

"You're always hungry." Marge poked him in the arm. "Let's get some bagels and cream cheese for breakfast."

"Breakfast? You mean we're skipping dinner?"

"Of course not," Hal reassured him. "How about pizza? They say New York pizza is like no other."

Trish flagged a cab down, and after a short ride they found a pizza place.

"That *was* good," David remarked after everyone had stuffed themselves.

Trish smiled at the grin on her brother's face. Only food could bring that look. But all the way back on the train she thought about the pills she'd seen her father take throughout the day. Since when did he take so many pills, and what were they all for?

CHAPTER 13

On the train returning to Belmont, Hal dozed. He had also napped when the tour bus stopped at St. John's Cathedral, and again when they toured Chinatown. Trish was glad he had made it through the day. Now he looked as if he had stretched his limit.

The next morning, when Trish and David returned to the hotel after morning works, Hal was up and dressed.

"Dad?" Trish gathered courage to broach the subject that was bothering her.

Hal looked up from the newspaper he was reading. "What is it, Tee? You sound awfully serious."

"What are all those pills you've been taking?"

Hal laid the paper in his lap. "Mostly pain pills."

Trish felt her heart clench in her chest. "Is it that bad?"

"If I don't take the pills it is. The doctors told me to be sure to stay on top of it. The body has to fight harder to heal itself when the pain is too severe."

Trish sank down on the floor beside her father's chair. "Is that why you sleep so much? The pills make you sleepy?"

"Somewhat. But fighting cancer, or any illness for that matter, takes a lot of energy."

"Why didn't you tell me?" She leaned her head on his knees.

"Oh, Tee. You've had so much on your mind lately. The racing, Spitfire's injury, then the accident. I didn't want you to worry about me."

Marge sat down on the arm of the chair. "That's my job. You both know how good I am at worrying. Besides, taking care of your father gives me something to do."

Trish smiled. "Isn't there anything I can do?"

Hal smoothed Trish's hair, and his love for her warmed her spirit. "Keep praying, Tee. Enjoy the moments we can spend together. We're all doing what we can. The rest is in God's hands."

Trish nodded, but secretly she thought, *Seems to me God isn't doing too well right now.*

Her nagger cut in, *You haven't been praying for your dad very much.*

Trish had a hard time ignoring that accusation. It was true. She hadn't been praying consistently, and she hadn't been reviewing her verses, either. Would she *ever* learn?

"What else haven't you told me?" Trish asked her dad.

Hal was silent until Trish looked up at him. Had he fallen asleep?

"Nothing that I can think of. You know I've always tried to be honest with you kids."

Trish nodded. She knew he had.

"All I know, Tee, is that Jesus promised to never leave us alone. No matter what happens." He lifted her chin with one finger. "Do you believe that?"

Trish nodded. She couldn't speak.

"Then we just take one day at a time."

"Speaking of time—" Marge looked at her watch.

"We need to get David to the airport. You coming along, Trish?"

"No, I better hit the books again. There won't be much time this next week."

David set his suitcase on a chair. "See you Tuesday, Tee."

"Yeah. Tell Rhonda hi for me. And Brad. You've got his present?"

David nodded. "In the suitcase. Anything else?"

"No. Just have fun for me."

After her family had left, Trish stared for a long time at her history book without seeing the print. Vancouver seemed so far away. It was hard to believe that she'd really go back to school after the Belmont, like nothing had ever happened. She propped her chin on her knee. Her life had changed in the last few months. Would it ever be the same again? Did she want to go back to her old life?

That night Trish made sure she spent time praying—not just the quickies she'd been saying. She thanked God for taking care of all of them, for guarding them during the accident, for helping them win the two races. When she begged Him to make her dad better again, the tears slipped down her cheeks. "I *need* my dad," she whispered.

Just before she fell asleep, a new thought came to her mind. Even though she was unhappy with God, it wasn't like last year. She couldn't shut Him out. God seemed more real right now.

———

God was in her first thoughts in the morning, too. Trish shook her head. Could she call God sneaky? It seemed to fit. The thought stayed with her all the way to the track.

"Breeze her three furlongs," Patrick said as he tossed Trish into the saddle on Monday morning. "Don't let her drift out on you and be sure you pull her down right away."

"She doesn't seem to mind the blinders." Trish stroked the filly's fiery red neck and smoothed her mane.

"Let's see what happens if another horse runs with you," Patrick said. "If all goes okay, we'll work her out of the starting gate after that."

Sarah's Pride seemed to know something was up. She jigged sideways until Patrick demanded she behave. Once on the track, she played crab, trotting sideways again. Trish straightened her out once, then again. The third time she pulled the filly to a stop.

"Now you're gonna stand here until you can behave." Trish refused to let up until the filly stood still for an entire minute. Sarah's Pride got the hint. Trish wasn't putting up with any more shenanigans.

When Trish turned the filly at the far turn, she nudged her into a jog. With the release of the reins at the mile-and-a-quarter post, the filly leaped forward. She ran straight and true, ignoring the other horses on the track.

"Thatta girl," Trish chanted as she pulled the horse back to a canter after they'd flashed past Patrick and his stopwatch. Trish didn't need the grin on Patrick's face to tell her they'd done well.

The filly snorted and fidgeted in the starting gate. When the gate swung open she reared instead of starting clean. But by the fourth break she settled down. Her twitching ears seemed to focus on Trish's commands and the break was clean and fast.

"Good, girl. That's the way," Trish praised her mount.

"I'm thinkin' one more day at this'll do it." Patrick held the reins and removed the hood. "There now. See you back at the barn."

When she was finished with Sarah's Pride, Trish led Spitfire clear around the barn and then out to a rail-fenced, grassy area by their barn to graze. He walked the distance, head up, eyes bright, without a limp.

"Enjoy." Trish loosened the lead so Spitfire could put his head down and graze. The sun sparkled on his blue-black hide. The cicadas chorused in the trees while Spitfire munched grass. Somewhere, someone had been mowing grass; the sweet perfume of it floated on the slight breeze. Trish breathed it in. She enjoyed the sights, sounds and smells of Belmont in early summer. Five days to go.

Studying for the rest of the day did not come near the top of Trish's wish list—but she did it anyway. Finals were scheduled for the week after they got home. She didn't need her mother to remind her of that.

Tuesday morning Patrick saddled Spitfire. "Just walk him down past the stands and back. The mile and a half is too far right now."

Spitfire walked carefully, a bit stiff-legged. But he didn't limp. As soon as they returned to the barn, Patrick applied the ice pack again.

That afternoon Trish and Patrick schooled Sarah's Pride. They followed the line of horses down through the underpass and up to the saddling paddock.

Shade and sunlight dappled the white-roofed, open-air stalls. Huge elm and oak trees created a park around the circular walking lane where spectators stood on brick risers to watch the pre-post parade. White metal fences with cutouts of running horses edged the tiers.

A cast-iron statue of Secretariat in full speed graced the center, surrounded by red geraniums. A white wrought-iron chair gave visitors to the legend of racing a place to rest. Beyond, rose the three-story arched windows of the Clubhouse.

Trish was having a falling-jaw attack again. The place was incredible. She could tell Belmont Park cost money—lots of money. Racing in New York was *big* business.

She chuckled to herself. It all compared to Portland Meadows like the sun to the moon. Sarah's Pride nudged her in the back as if to say, "quit gawking and start walking."

That evening David returned from his trip to Vancouver. Trish studied again while her parents went to the airport. When David walked into the suite, he was carrying a thin package under his arm.

"How was the graduation? Did Brad get his scholarship? Did you see Rhonda? How's Miss Tee?" Trish bubbled over with questions. "For me?" she asked as David handed her the package.

"Open it. Then I'll answer all your questions."

Trish carefully untied the curled crimson and gold ribbon, then removed the brown wrapping paper. Two pieces of posterboard were taped together to make a huge card. It depicted a broken-down, old black nag stumbling across the page. A square bandage covered one haunch; the lower lip hung nearly to the sprung knees. A woman jockey sat on the swayback, her legs clapped to the bony ribs.

Trish giggled. "Did Rhonda draw this?" The caption read ON TO BELMONT. Inside the card, the horse had shaped up considerably. It held a rose in its teeth and the jockey waved a trophy. The inside words read, "Trish did it her way. Congratulations!" The signatures of Prairie students covered every inch of the inside and back of the card. Trish turned it over and back again, sniffling as she read. The teachers had signed it, too. In the right lower corner, Rhonda had drawn a red heart and signed her name across it.

Trish handed the card to her mother while she went to get a tissue.

"Can you believe it?" she said, sinking into a chair, her legs dangling over the arm. "Wow." She blew her nose again.

Hal and Marge chuckled as they looked at the card, then handed it back to Trish. "You'll need a couple of hours just to read all the messages," Marge said. "They must have worked on it for days."

"I wish Brad and Rhonda were here. Remember when they showed up for our first race? They were whooping and hollering; I was afraid the security guards were going to throw them out. Then I was afraid they wouldn't." She shook her head. "Guess I don't embarrass so easily anymore." She looked at the inside of the card again. Brad had signed his name on the end of the horse's nose.

"So how was graduation?" Trish asked again.

David told her everything he could remember, and then Trish prompted him with more questions. "Seems like we've been away from home forever," he finally said. "Miss Tee and Double-Diamond have both grown some. Poor old Caesar thinks we've all deserted him. He wouldn't let me out of his sight." David stretched both arms above his head. "I'm beat. Talk about a fast trip."

He turned to Trish. "How's Spitfire doing?"

"I walked him today."

"Do you think you'll race him?" David looked to his father.

"Who knows." Hal leaned back in his chair. "He favors the leg, even though he walked without limping. Patrick is doing all he can, packs and ultrasound. We'll keep going like we're in the running, and decide on Friday."

Trish huddled in her chair. Friday. Three days away. Was there any chance they could do it?

———

On Wednesday morning Trish walked Spitfire again. She trotted the filly to loosen her up. Sarah's Pride would have her chance in the afternoon.

In the jockey room, Trish studied while waiting for the race. *I must be getting better disciplined*, Trish thought. *I can study anywhere.* She glared at the new list of assignments David had brought her. She'd *better* be able to study anywhere with all she had to do. She tapped her pencil thoughtfully. Her mother had only mentioned studying. Maybe she'd given up nagging.

Or maybe you're doing much better on your own, and she thinks so, too, Trish's little voice reminded her.

Or she's so worried about your dad, she doesn't have time to think about your studies. Her nagger had to get in his two-cents worth.

Trish glanced up at the monitor. They were running the third race. She finished dressing, ready to walk out the door when the call came to weigh in.

Hal, Patrick, and David waited for her in the paddock. Sarah's Pride pranced her way right into the hearts of the spectators.

"That's Tricia Evanston!" someone exclaimed.

"Hey, Trish, how about an autograph?" A man held out his program and a pen.

Trish signed her name with a flourish. Two other programs appeared in front of her.

"Sure hope Spitfire will be ready to run." One woman shook her head. "Shame to come so far and have to scratch."

"Yes, ma'am," Trish agreed. "We need all the prayers we can get."

A tiny little lady with snow-white hair reached out and patted Trish's arm. "I've been praying for him, and your father, too. God hears us."

Trish covered the woman's hand with her own. "Thank you very much."

At the call for riders up, Trish joined the men walking the flame-red filly around the paddock. She shook her head, amazed at the intricate ways God used to get through to her.

Patrick gave her a leg up. "Now, lass, keep in mind that ye carry that whip for a reason. Use it if you have to. This girl needs a win bad. And it wouldn't be a-hurtin' you, either."

Trish fingered the whip. She hated to use it. But she nodded down at Patrick. "You know best."

Hal nodded. "He does."

Sarah's Pride put on a real show on the Parade to Post. She danced and snorted. As they cantered back past the grandstand, she kept trying to race her pony rider. But when the gate swung open and the race began, she was content to run with the field. Two horses broke away and lengthened their lead.

Trish held the filly steady around the turn, keeping her from drifting to the outside. Down the stretch she hollered in the filly's ear and shifted her weight—anything to get the horse running harder. Finally she went to the whip.

Sarah's Pride leaped forward at the crack and drove between the two front-runners. Trish smacked her again. Neck and neck, the three pounded for the wire. One more thwack and the filly surged forward, one long line from nose to streaming tail.

"Photo finish!" the announcer and tote board declared at once.

Trish cantered on part-way around the track, then turned and trotted back to the winner's circle. The three contenders walked around in circles while the rest of the field were stripped of their tack and led off to the barns.

"And that's number five, Sarah's Pride. Owned by Hal Evanston and ridden by Tricia Evanston. Ladies and gentlemen, that was the closest race I've ever called. Place goes to number three, with number one a show. The three were only separated by whiskers."

As the announcer spoke, Trish turned the filly to face the grandstand for the applause. "That's for you, girl. See how good it feels?" The filly stood, head up, accepting her due. "That's what this is all about, you know—winning." The filly nodded.

Patrick took the reins and led them into the winner's circle. The aisle led past red and white baskets of flowers, and the circle was decorated with potted trees and plants, also with blooms of red and white.

"You think she got the idea?" Hal asked as they posed for pictures.

"We'll know for sure next race, but I think so." Trish leaped to the ground and stripped off her saddle so she could weigh in.

"You and Patrick did a fine job with her," Hal said to Trish after David had led the filly off to the detention barn for testing.

"Thanks, but it took a special eye to choose her. You know how to pick 'em, Dad." She tucked her helmet under her arm and rubbed carefully at the edge of her injured eye. The bruise had faded to an ugly green and yellow. "You know what's neat? That purse paid for her."

Hal pulled both Trish and her mother close. "How about some lunch up in the Clubhouse?"

Trish looked down at her dirty silks. "Like this?"

Hal stepped back to take a look. "Okay, you get five minutes to change. We'll go get a table. And tonight we'll go see the Empire State Building—after dark."

Trish trotted off happily. Why couldn't things just stay like this?

CHAPTER 14

Spectacular was too small a word to describe the view. Trish leaned on the metal railing around the top floor of the Empire State Building, looking toward upper Manhattan. Central Park lay like an oblong black hole between the lighted streets and tall buildings. Skyscrapers glittered against the night sky. A man next to them knew the city, and Trish listened as he pointed out the various buildings to his companion.

Walking around the observation deck, the Evanstons looked toward the downtown financial district. The twin World Trade towers dominated the skyline.

"There are so many buildings, and they're all so different," Trish commented, leaning her chin on her hands against the railing. "What do you suppose it's like up here in a windstorm?"

"The building sways," Hal answered.

"Wow!"

"It feels like it's swaying now," Marge said. "Some of these tiles move when you step on them, and I'm sure the building is moving."

"Awww, Mom," David teased her. "You just need something to worry about."

"Well, worriers have *very* vivid imaginations," Marge acknowledged. She clung to Hal's arm. "So I'm entitled.

Don't you think we've seen enough now? We've been around three times."

"In a minute." Hal laid his hand over hers. "Listen. You can hear the roar of the city clear up here. Just think of all the people crammed on this small island."

"Think I'll stick to the country," David observed. "I thought Portland was a pretty big city, until now."

Trish looked up. White moths danced in the spotlights. Higher up, the spire flashed red lights. A helicopter clattered past, then swung out over the Hudson River. Trish dragged her feet back to the first elevator. The building was so tall it took two elevators to return them to street level.

On the way out they read the signs and studied displays that told the story of the Empire State Building. For many years it had been the tallest building in the world. Now the Sears Tower in Chicago was the largest. A plaque listed the names of construction workers who had won awards for their skills.

"What a nice thing to do," Marge said. "It's easy to forget the contribution that everyday people make in this world."

"Our name is on a trophy or two," Trish said. "And Spitfire will be famous forever."

"That's true," Marge agreed. "And your name has gone down in the annals of thoroughbred racing, too. How does it feel to be world-famous at sixteen?"

Trish tipped her head to the side and rolled her lips together. "I don't *feel* any different than I did before the Derby. I'm still the same old me." She raised her arms and twirled in a circle. "Do I look any different?"

"Nope. Just as dopey as ever." David ducked before Trish could punch his shoulder. "I know one thing that's different."

"What's that?" Hal asked as he guided them all toward the exit.

"We have a lot more money than we did. Those purses we've won take the pressure off, at least for a while."

"True," Hal acknowledged.

David flagged down a cab. After they'd all climbed inside, Hal continued, "We'll do things like pay off the mortgage on the farm, make some investments, set money aside for college for each of you . . ."

Trish flinched at the mention of college. She wanted to race, not study.

"Just think, you can go to whatever college you wish." Marge settled back against the seat. "And not have to worry about money."

"What would you like?" Hal took Marge's hand. "As a sort of reward for all the stress we've put you through?"

Marge thought a moment. "A new car, I guess. The poor old station wagon has seen a lot of miles."

"How about a red convertible?" Trish muttered under her breath. David snorted, and Hal swallowed a chuckle.

A smile tugged at the corners of Marge's mouth. "Sure. Three red convertibles sitting in our front yard . . ." She laughed lightly. "The neighbors will think we've gone into the car business." She shook her head. "No, make mine something with a solid top. I don't want to have to worry about water dripping in during the winter. One of those mini-vans would be nice."

Trish tried to hear the conversation without missing all the sights. They'd just crossed the Brooklyn Bridge.

"And what would you like, Tee?" Hal asked.

"More horses," she answered without a thought. "We

could go to the January yearling sale at Santa Anita. And breed all the mares to better stallions."

Hal raised his hand. "Okay, okay. We get the picture."

"What about you, Davey boy?" Trish asked.

"I already have what I wanted—thanks to you." He tapped Trish's knee. "A decent car. College was my next dream. What can I say?"

Trish felt a warm glow of pride and deep happiness surround her family. "What about you, Dad?"

"Having money has never been a big issue with me . . ." He put his arm around Marge. ". . . with us. But knowing that all of you are provided for takes a big load off my mind. I think I'd like to buy something for the church—maybe a bus or a van. David, why don't you look into that when we get home."

Trish rested her head on her father's shoulder. *What we need most can't be bought. God, please make my dad better.*

Hal leaned on David and Marge for support on the way up to their suite. While he made a joke of it, Trish could tell by the way his steps faltered that he was exhausted. And the post position draw was in the morning.

Patrick had Trish walk Spitfire around the entire track at morning works.

"I don't think he'll make it," she heard one railbird say. "He ain't run all week."

Trish leaned forward to rub Spitfire's neck. "A lot he knows about it," she whispered in the horse's ear. She relaxed in the saddle and let her feet dangle below the stirrups. "You just keep getting better. We'll show 'em."

Reporters asked the same question they always asked. "Will he run?" One of the more ambitious ones walked beside Trish on their way back to the barn. "What do you think your father will do?"

"We're just taking a day at a time. We have up to the morning of the race to scratch if we have to." Trish had made the comment so many times she felt like a stuck needle on a record.

When she walked into the dining room for the post position draw, Trish had a surprise. Adam and Martha Finley stood talking with her mother and father.

"Hear you brought that filly in by a whisker," Adam said after he greeted her. "I didn't think you could do it."

"Patrick suggested the blinkers. I think she'll do all right now. She found out what winning is all about, and she liked the applause." Trish turned to greet Martha and found herself enveloped in a warm hug.

"I knew you could do it," she whispered in Trish's ear. "You've got that magic touch."

"Thanks." Trish hugged her back. "You always make me feel so good."

The crowd quieted as the officials filed to the front of the room. Each person had been given a list of the seven horses entered in the race. By now Trish could pick out the owners, trainers, and jockey for each horse. The groups huddled together, waiting for the program to begin.

Nomatterwhat drew the post position. A cheer went up from his group. Equinox drew number six. Others were called; number two, number four.

Spitfire's name was next to last. "Number seven. Spitfire in gate seven."

"Right next to Equinox again," Trish mumbled. "At least we won't have to wait in the gate while the rest of them calm down."

With the drawing of the last number, the ceremony

was over. Before the officials had left the podium, a reporter had his mike in front of Hal's face.

"Will Spitfire be well enough to run?"

His question lacked originality, in Trish's estimation. She mouthed the words along with her father. "We are taking . . ."

"Has the colt been limping? Will you breeze him tomorrow?"

Hal shook his head to both questions. "I'm sorry I can't be of more help. We just don't know for sure."

"Tough break, to come so far and have an accident on the turnpike."

The Shipsons joined the group, and the reporter left. "I hear congratulations are in order for you, young lady." Mr. Shipson extended his hand. "Both for winning with the filly and bringing ours in, too. Have you thought about racing in Kentucky next year?"

Trish looked to see if her mother had heard the comment.

"Don't get your hopes up," Finley put in. "We asked her first. And California is closer to Washington than Kentucky is."

Trish caught Patrick's eye and he winked at her. She glanced at her father. He was slumped in the chair, and looked as though his shoulders were too heavy to hold up.

When her mother, Martha Finley, and Bernice Shipson suggested a shopping trip, Trish turned it down. Although the idea of shopping in New York City was tempting, Trish had something she had to do and this would give her the opportunity.

"I need to study, and Patrick may have me walk Spitfire this evening," she said. "But thanks, anyway. Have fun, Mom. Why don't you buy yourself something nice—

like a new dress for the winner's circle." She smiled. "You haven't had a new dress for a long time."

Marge studied her daughter suspiciously. "Take care of your dad, then. And study hard. We probably won't be back until late." She kissed Hal. "Get some rest now, okay?"

Hal nodded. "You have a good time, Marge. And take your daughter's suggestion."

Trish drove her father back to the hotel and helped him to his room.

"Thanks, Tee." Hal sank down on the bed. "I know I'll feel better after I sleep awhile." He reached for his pills and took a couple with a glass of water from the nightstand.

He lay down, and Trish untied his shoes and slipped them off. "Are you hurting bad?"

"Just staying on top of it." He stretched out, and Trish pulled the sheet up. "Right now I could use those eagles' wings."

Trish smiled, but said nothing. Within seconds Hal was asleep.

He looks like an old man, the thought struck Trish with the force of a mule kick. *Where has my real father gone?*

Later that afternoon, when Hal was awake, Trish went out and bought fried chicken and took it back to the hotel.

When she and her father were seated at the table, she cleared her throat and began, "Remember last night in the taxi when you asked what I wanted to do with some of the money?"

Hal nodded. "Yes?"

"Well, what I really want—" She paused and looked her father straight in the eye. "Is there any place—like a hospital—that you could go for some other kind of treatment? Maybe some experimental stuff—something that would work better for you? We can afford it now. Even another country, if necessary." She finished quickly before the tears choked her up. "Have you thought about that?"

"No, not really. Since they found the new tumors all I could think of was getting back to you—to the tracks. How about if when we get home we talk to the doctors? They've had time now to study my situation, and may have some new recommendations. Actually, they weren't too happy with me when I walked out on them."

"Walked out on them?"

"That's right. We had to get back here."

Trish nodded. "But you'll really look into it then?"

"Yes, Trish, I promise."

———

Trish fell asleep that night with one thought on her mind. Tomorrow they would decide. Would Spitfire race on Saturday or not?

Friday morning dawned with a drizzle. Trish alternately walked and trotted Spitfire around the track. She could feel a difference in him. He seemed to both walk and trot on his tiptoes. He was ready to run.

When Trish brought Sarah's Pride back to the barn after an easy gallop of the entire track, she could feel water dripping off the end of her nose. She sniffed as she leaped to the ground.

Before she knew what was happening, strong arms circled her waist and whirled her around in a strong hug.

"Red!" She looked into his face. "You came!" She hugged him again. "What took you so long?"

"Is that all you can say—" Red nearly squished her

hand, "after I drove most of the night to get here?"

Trish looked at David and Patrick who stood nearby. She could feel the heat begin to rise from her toes up. By the time her neck and cheeks were hot, she felt as if she could light up the barn. Somehow the day didn't seem gray anymore.

Patrick winked at her, and David rolled his eyes.

Red broke the tension by asking, "You about ready for some breakfast?"

"Uh—yeah—maybe—" Trish took a deep breath and looked at David. "I'd better help with the chores first, though."

"Aw, go on. We're almost done. Catch up with you over at the kitchen."

Trish couldn't ignore the fact that Red was still holding her hand. The tingle up her arm made her throat dry. But that didn't keep her from talking. And laughing—for no reason at all. By the time they walked into the cafeteria they'd caught up on each other's news, and Trish felt back to normal—sort of.

After breakfast Hal met them all back at the barn. "Well, what do you think, Patrick? Is it a go—or no?"

Trish felt as if her heart were in her throat. At least it was pounding about five times faster than normal. She watched Patrick's face, trying to out-guess him.

"Well, we haven't galloped him. I don't know what that might do to his leg." He paused, as if studying something on the wall.

Trish wanted to scream at him to hurry.

"But there's been no heat or swelling for the last couple of days. The lad walks like he's on top o' the world."

Hal studied his hands. "If we run him, we could lame him for life, right?" He raised his head and looked at Patrick.

Patrick started to shake his head, then frowned. "Not sure I'd go quite that far. Could take him some time to heal though."

Trish chewed on the cuticle of her thumb. She felt sick to her stomach. Would they *ever* make the decision? She glanced at David. He was clipping his fingernails—a sure sign he was worried.

Looks to me like running in the Belmont is more important to you than Spitfire's leg, Trish's little nagger spoke out of nowhere.

Trish gritted her teeth. *I just want to know what we're going to do. That's all.*

Right?

She heard a nicker down the long, sandy aisle. Spitfire stuck his head over the gate and answered.

"If you want my true, gut opinion," Patrick broke the silence, "I say go for it. I think he can do it."

Hal let out a sigh that sounded as if he hadn't breathed for the last five minutes. "Then that's what we'll do."

Thank you, God! Thank you, thank you, thank you! Trish jumped up and down and ran the few steps to stand in front of Spitfire. She placed her hands on both sides of his face and looked him straight in the eye. "We're gonna run tomorrow, old man. And it's gonna take all we got."

Spitfire blew in Trish's face, then dropped his head against her chest. Running was tomorrow. Right now he wanted a good scratching. Trish obliged him.

That night Hal took their extended family, which included Red, Patrick, and the Finleys, out for a steak dinner. "We have lots to celebrate," he told them as they sat around the table. "Whether we win or lose tomorrow we've given it all we've got. What more can anyone do?"

"To Trish and Spitfire." Adam raised his glass of iced tea. As the others joined in the toast, Trish raised her glass, too. Her butterflies took a flying leap at the same time. A toast of their own, perhaps?

Tomorrow afternoon the final race for the Triple Crown would take place. Trish stared at her plate when the waitress placed it in front of her. The steak had sounded so good—*before* the inner aerial display. She picked at her food, moving it around her plate while enjoying the conversation around the table.

That is, until her father choked. He coughed and gagged and covered his mouth with a napkin. When he was unable to stop coughing, Marge thumped his back. David was on his feet, ready to apply the Heimlich maneuver if necessary.

"Dad, are you all right?" Panic made Trish's voice sound shrill.

Hal shook his head and coughed again. This time he blinked and breathed deeply. "Yes, I got it out." He coughed again, more softly this time, but couldn't seem to stop altogether.

When he finally wiped his mouth with his napkin, Trish saw a smear of blood across his lips and cheek. "Dad!"

Hal looked at her, then down at his napkin. "Oh, God, no." He wiped his mouth again and took a sip of water.

"I think we better get you to a hospital and check this out," Marge laid her hand on his shoulder. "The rest of you finish your dinner. We'll probably be back at the hotel before you are."

Trish shoved her chair back so hard it crashed to the floor. "I'll drive."

"No, I will." David took Trish by the arm. "Come on."

"Do you want me to call an ambulance?" the maitre d' asked.

"No, just tell me where the nearest hospital is." David listened carefully to the instructions.

"Right, go three blocks, turn left, go one mile and left again at the sign to Mercy Hospital."

David almost shoved Trish ahead of him. "I'll bring the car around. You help Mom with Dad."

Hal seemed better in the car. He breathed carefully, as though afraid a deep breath would start the coughing again.

"They'll just check me over and send me back to the hotel," he grumbled. "All this over a piece of meat caught in my throat."

It seemed as if they'd been waiting for hours when a nurse came into the Emergency Room fifteen minutes later. She led the way to a white-curtained cubicle, and they all trooped in

The nurse patted the table and looked at Hal. "Sit right up here and the doctor will be with you in a moment." Then she picked up a clipboard and started asking questions.

Now I know what Mom felt like after my accidents, Trish thought. The questions seemed to go on forever.

A tall man with iron-gray hair parted the curtains. "I'm Doctor Silverstein. The restaurant called and said you'd choked on a piece of meat." As he spoke, he took out his stethoscope and applied it to Hal's chest. "And you had blood on your napkin after that."

Trish clenched her fists until she could feel the nails digging into her palms. *Hurry up!*

"Why don't you young people step into the waiting

room? I'll let you know as soon as I find anything."

Trish shook her head stubbornly, but David took her by the arm.

"It's okay, Trish," Hal said. "I'm not going anywhere."

Trish flipped through a magazine, not seeing the words or pictures. All she *could* see was the blood on the napkin.

David slouched in the chair beside her. Then he sat up and leaned forward, dropping his head and clasping his hands. After getting up and walking around the room, he sat down again to repeat the pattern.

Trish's nerves couldn't have been more frazzled if someone had stood at a blackboard and dragged their nails across it.

Hearing footsteps in the hall, Trish looked up immediately. Marge came to sit in the chair beside her. "They've decided to keep your father overnight for observation and some X-rays. Let's go get him settled."

"Overnight? What's wrong?" Trish blinked to keep the tears back.

"The doctor thinks there's fluid in your father's lungs." Marge fiddled with her purse. "The X-rays will tell us more."

When they arrived at the door to Hal's room, he was already in bed. Trish flew into his outstretched arms. "It's okay," he murmured, stroking her hair. "You and David go on back to the hotel and get some sleep."

"No, I want to stay here." Trish raised her tear-stained face. "I can sleep in that chair."

"No, that's my chair," Marge said, standing beside the bed. She put her hand on Trish's shoulder. "We're not that far away from the hotel. If you need us, just call."

"Besides, you have to be at your best tomorrow," Hal

reminded her. "We'll let them check me out, and I'll see you before you head for the jockey room."

Trish could hear the rattle in her father's chest. She'd heard it before. Back in September, when all this started.

"Don't worry, I'll be better in the morning." Hal kissed Trish's forehead. "And remember that I love you."

Trish bit her lip and nodded. "Me, too. Good-night." She whirled and dashed out of the room.

David hurried after her without saying a word.

Worry nagged at Trish all the way back to the hotel. *Worry!* That's what got her mother into so much trouble. Why was it so easy to say don't worry, and so hard not to?

She went to her father's room at the hotel and picked up the carved eagle. As she crawled into bed, she pictured the verses on her wall at home. She needed some promises. "Be not afraid . . ." That was a good one for tonight. "I will never leave you . . ."

"Please, heavenly Father, take care of *my* father tonight. I love him so much, and I know you do, too. The race is tomorrow. He needs to be there. I need him to be there. Thank you for being with us." With Trish's "amen" she was asleep.

In the morning she awoke with a start. Her heart leaped. *This is the day!* She checked the clock. It was just seven. After digging the phone book out of the drawer, she looked up Hospitals and ran her finger down the m's. Mercy Hospital. She dialed the number.

"Room 736, please."

The phone rang. And rang. There was no answer.

CHAPTER 15

David had awakened instantly. "Call the nurse's station," he told her.

Trish's teeth chattered. She felt as if she were standing in a deep freeze.

"M-my father—Hal Evanston," she stuttered. "There was no answer to the phone in his room."

"They've taken him down to X-ray," the nurse's voice soothed. "Your mother went with him. Should I have her call you when she can?"

"No." Trish shook her head methodically. "No, we'll call later. Just tell them that we called—please."

"Of course."

Trish put down the receiver, and a band of ice circled her heart.

———

When she and David arrived at the track, reporters swarmed the area.

"I can't talk to them," Trish told David pleadingly. "Not right now. You and Patrick handle it."

Working the horses brought a measure of peace to Trish's mind. Her father had promised to be at the track before she left for the jockey room. He always kept his promises.

But he didn't come. Nine o'clock passed. Nine-thirty.

David called the hospital again, and when he returned to tell Trish their father was down for more tests, she said, "I'm going to the hospital."

"You can't. There's no time." David grabbed her by the shoulders. "You heard what Dad said. He'll be here. You just concentrate on the job you have to do. We've come too far to mess up now."

"But David—"

"He's right, lass," Patrick rejoined. "You know what your dad would want you to do." He set down a can of saddle soap. "I know it's a long time to wait up there, but we'll get any message to you that's necessary."

"Come on, Trish." Red took her hand. "I'll walk you over."

"Me, too." David picked up her school books. "Wouldn't want you to be bored."

Trish stopped in front of Spitfire. "Sure would rather stay with you, fella." She rubbed his ears and smoothed his forelock. "You get ready now, you hear? This is the big one." Spitfire sniffed her pockets, lipped the carrot off her palm, and licked her cheek for good measure. Trish threw her arms around his neck and buried her face in his mane. Her shoulders shook but no sound came.

David and Red waited patiently.

Trish wiped her eyes and swallowed hard. "Okay, let's go." Together they turned and headed down the street to the Clubhouse.

"I'll let you know as soon as I hear anything, I promise," David assured her outside the jockey room.

Trish nodded. She took her books, squeezed Red's hand, and stumbled into the jockey room—to wait.

Her mind was a jumble of prayers, promises, and

worry. When she tried to relax with deep breathing, her insides joined the jumble.

At noon Trish called the hospital herself. Her mother answered the phone on the second ring.

"Yes, Trish, we're on our way. The doctors are having a fit but your father refuses to listen. Here, you want to talk to him?"

Trish strangled the receiver with her hand. Her throat clenched so tight she didn't think she'd be able to talk. But her father's welcome voice broke the dam for her.

"It's okay, Tee," she finally heard him say. "Come on now, you'll be all right. We're coming, but I may not make it to the saddling paddock. Look for me in the winner's circle."

"Dad, I'm so scared."

"I know. But it's okay. Just go out there and ride. Go for the glory."

Trish sniffed and fumbled in her pocket for a tissue. "Thanks. I love you."

"I know that. And I love you too. See you soon."

What did her father mean by soon? The fifth race came and went. Trish began her pre-race routine. She sprayed her goggles, polished her boots, brushed her hair. She even added extra deodorant—she'd need it today for sure. Then she was down on the floor doing stretches.

When the call came she was dressed and ready. "This is it, God. For *your* glory." She walked out the door and over to the men's jockey room to weigh in.

"Mom and Dad are on their way," David called, as Trish walked with the other jockeys down the incline to the saddling paddock.

"I know. I talked to them." Trish stepped in front of

Spitfire and leaned her forehead against his. "Well, fella, can you run a mile and a half today? We gotta do it—for Dad."

The noise of the crowd receded. It was as though there were a crystal bell around Trish's head. She could see what was going on, but the noise and the pressure were at bay. She was in a literal sea of peace.

"You'll do it, lass." Patrick gave her a leg up at the call.

With David and Patrick on either side, they followed the rest of the field up the incline and under the Clubhouse.

The last bugle notes of Parade to Post hovered on the slight breeze as Trish picked up her pony rider on the edge of the track. The track was listed as fast, the sun warm but not hot.

As they stepped onto the track, Trish heard her father's voice in her mind: *Remember, you're a winner. And winners never quit.* She leaned forward and stroked Spitfire's neck.

"They're cheering for you," she crooned, acknowledging the applause of the crowd. Then they were chanting, "Spitfire—Spitfire—Spitfire."

For one brief moment Trish wanted to turn and run. But she looked between Spitfire's ears at the track ahead. *I can do all things through Christ who strengthens me.* The verse put steel in her spine. She squared her shoulders and let the thunder of the crowd set her blood to pumping. *I can do all things—.* They cantered back past the crowd toward the starting gates.

Equinox was typically obnoxious. He didn't get any better with another race. Trish shook her head. They'd never let a horse get away with that kind of behavior on their farm. Spitfire waited patiently for his turn. He entered the gate and settled for the break.

The shot. The gate clanged open.

"They're off!"

Spitfire broke clean and settled into an easy stride. He ran, head up, ears pricked, as if they were out for a joyride. He and Trish seemed of one mind as they let two others set the pace. Patrick had reminded Trish to lay back and let the others wear themselves out. The real race would begin after the mile marker.

Trish loosened the reins. Spitfire snorted and flew past the third-place runner. He took the rail, two lengths behind the two dueling for the lead. Going into the turn it was Who Sez and Nomatterwhat, neck and neck. They pounded out of the turn and Who Sez faltered.

Spitfire passed him as if the gray were standing still. Now it was Nomatterwhat and Spitfire, just like in the last two races. Only now Nomatterwhat led by two lengths.

At the mile-and-a-quarter pole Trish crouched tight against Spitfire's neck, making herself as small as possible to cut the wind. "Okay, fella, this is it," she urged him forward. Her arms and legs lifted the horse onward. Stride for stride they gained on the lead.

Trish could hear the stands going wild. Her heart thundered with Spitfire's heaving grunts. Neck and neck for two strides and Spitfire began to pull away. Ahead by a nose, by a neck. Nomatterwhat disappeared from their view. They flashed across the finish line, ahead by a length. Trish raised her arm. Victory. Spitfire had won the Triple Crown!

Tears made rivulets down Trish's dusty face. "You did it! We did it!" She raised her face to the heavens. "Thank you, God. We did it!" She turned and cantered back to stand her horse in front of the Clubhouse crowd.

Applause rolled over them in waves. Spitfire stood, sides heaving but head up accepting the accolades like the king he was. Trish turned him toward the winner's circle. She felt him falter, then walk carefully as though he were in pain.

A crowd surged in and around the winner's circle. Huge cameras eyed them from every angle. Trish searched the crowd, looking for only one face. When she couldn't find her father, she started to dismount.

"No, lass." Patrick grabbed the reins.

"You can't fail him now," David hissed at her. "Let's just get through the ceremony."

Trish blinked back the tears and smiled at the Finleys and the Shipsons. She smiled when the cameramen asked her to, and raised her arms so they could drape the blanket of white carnations across her lap and Spitfire's withers. She smiled again. Her cheeks felt as if they were cracked.

As the cameras flashed again and the announcer began his spiel, Trish heard another voice. This one from the man she loved above all others—her father. *I have fought the good fight, Tee. I have won my race. Remember that I love you.*

"Dad's gone, isn't he?" she asked David, searching for the truth in his eyes.

David nodded and reached up to grasp her hand. "They got a message to us after the race had started."

Trish leaned against Spitfire's neck, fighting the knife-thrust of the awful reality. *My father* . . . She pushed herself upright. Teeth clenched against the tears streaming down her face, Trish turned to face the cameras. With his life and his love her father had taught her courage. She raised her arm, the victory salute.

ACKNOWLEDGEMENTS

My special thanks to Mel Howell, head of security for the Maryland Racing Commission, for sharing his fund of racing knowledge and his time with us at Pimlico. Thanks too to all those friendly people who answered my questions at Belmont and Aquaduct. All of you helped make our New York trip a special event.